A NEW IMAGE
Debby Mayne

With her new attitude, Amy Mitchell sets out on an adventure to discover what she wants to do with her life. She meets Zachary Harper while working a temporary job at a car show. The attraction between them is evident from the very beginning, despite how hard they try to squelch it. Their biggest obstacle is that they come from two different worlds: Zachary is from a long line of auto mechanics; and Amy comes from Nashville blueblood.

Is it possible that these total opposites can find some common ground? Or will the differences in their upbringing keep them apart?

A NEW IMAGE

•

Debby Mayne

AVALON BOOKS
NEW YORK

This book is dedicated to Ginger Braund, Barbara Caldwell, Sherry Broome, and Trisha Osburn—all fabulous ladies who don't mind working hard for what they want.

Thanks to editors Erin Cartwright and Mira Son for giving me the opportunity to write this series. I'd also like to thank Kathy Carmichael, Kimberly Llewellyn, and Sandie Bricker for their continued support and friendship.

Chapter One

"Are you sure, Denise?" Amy said as she leaned against the counter. "I—I mean, I'll stay here until you find a replacement for me."

Denise offered a sincere smile. "Don't worry, Amy. The woman who used to help out has gotten her life back in order, and she wants her old job back. You need this."

"Yes, you're right," Amy admitted. "I really do need this."

"Besides, not only will you have lots of fun experiences, you'll figure out what you want to do with your life. That's how I knew I wanted my own business."

Denise was referring to working temp jobs for an agency in town. Amy knew that Denise had been

1

searching for something stable in life when she'd signed with the company that sent her out on different jobs every few weeks. It sounded like the ideal way to find her niche.

"Any idea where they're sending you first?" Denise asked.

Amy shrugged. "Carol told me to come to the office first thing Friday morning, and she'd give me an assignment then. I'm kind of limited because I don't type."

"You can always learn to type if that's something you want to do."

"Yes, you're right. And I just might do that."

Denise had taught Amy that if there was something she wanted, all she had to do was figure out a way to get it. Sometimes it meant being in the right place at the right time, and other times it meant learning something new. That can-do attitude had been just the thing to inspire Amy. She had a new attitude, thanks to Denise, and her new image brought it to life.

When her brother Andrew came into the shop, he smiled at Amy, then went over to Denise and gave her a hug. It warmed Amy's heart to see the newlyweds showing their love for each other. Maybe one day, she'd find the right man to spend the rest of her life with.

"How's it feel to walk out of here on your last day?" Andrew asked.

Amy rolled her eyes in that new way she'd learned from Phyllis, who taught her to vividly express herself, calling attention to her new makeup job. "It's not exactly like I'm never coming back."

Andrew chuckled. "This is true. Just don't get too carried away. I'm not sure I can handle my sister going corporate."

"Well, first, I'll have to find a corporation before I think of anything like that."

Denise nudged Andrew. "I have a feeling Amy will discover something she wants to do on her own. She's pretty independent, ya know."

Nodding, Andrew replied, "Yeah, I do know that now."

Amy enjoyed every minute of conversation about herself, something she'd shied away from in the past. But now she knew the comments were all complimentary, and she felt deserving.

"I can't hang around here all day," she finally said, backing toward the door. "I have things to do and appointments to keep."

"You go, girl," Denise said with a grin.

Amy winked and left the bookstore. She really did have a hair appointment with Connie. She wanted to look fresh for her new adventure.

"Don't you look like the picture of happiness?" Connie said as Amy sat down in the beauty shop chair. "This new image certainly agrees with you."

"Yes, it does. I'm just glad everyone was so nice and helpful."

Connie waved her comb around. "That's what friends are for." She paused for a moment to study

Amy, then said, "Okay, what'll it be? A light trim, or a completely new look?"

Amy chuckled. "I'm not ready for another new look. Why don't you just trim the ends and give it a little shape?"

"Okay," Connie said, a tiny note of disappointment in her voice. "Just don't stay with the same style too long, or you'll look dated."

The way Connie snipped her hair without a single worry impressed Amy. She was amazed at anyone who loved what she did day in and day out. Hopefully, she'd find something she could enjoy as much as Connie liked cutting hair.

On her way out, Amy paid and left a generous tip. "Thanks, Connie. Looks great."

"Let me know how it goes, sweetie. I want every detail."

"Trust me, I won't leave anything out."

Amy felt free as a bird as she walked down the street, almost as if she was floating on air. Her future was unknown, something that had frightened her in the past. But after meeting Denise and seeing how things could work out, she was exhilarated and eager to get started on her search for something to do with her life.

Andrew had given her a hard time in the beginning, but after he saw how much she wanted to "find herself," he was her biggest supporter. He even helped her convince their parents.

Her mother accepted the news right away, but her

father was a different story. At first, he bellowed, "You don't have to be in business, Amy. I've set up a trust for you, and you can do charity work, like your mother."

She'd argued, letting him know that it was important for her to know that she could support herself. And Andrew had agreed, explaining it in a way only he was able to do, telling their dad that this would help Amy grow into the kind of person she wanted to be. In other words, she needed this for self-respect. Their father had eventually given in and offered to help finance a new business.

"Only if you'll allow me to pay you back," Amy told him.

He didn't like that idea, either, but he conceded, saying he'd just put the money she paid him back into her trust fund. Amy knew he was acting out of love, so she didn't argue. Being rich wasn't all it was cracked up to be, but she couldn't very well do anything about it, so she didn't try.

So now, she had this wonderful new image, and she had an appointment to get her first assignment. Carol at the temporary job placement agency had told her she needed to learn some office skills; but in the meantime, she'd send her to all the sites where she could use her people skills, which had come from years of social competency lessons required by the upper crust in Nashville.

Denise had picked out an awesome red suit for her to wear on her first day. Never in a million years would she have chosen anything so loud if left to pick it out on her own, but she had to admit, red was her best color. Especially this bright tomato red.

She tried it on one more time before she got ready for bed. Amy loved living in the cottage, now that Denise and Andrew had gotten married. Denise had objected to moving into the mansion, but Amy was afraid to stay there alone, so she agreed. "Just until it sells," Denise had told her. "I want to get back in a real neighborhood as soon as possible."

Amy decided she'd start looking for a house of her own as soon as they had an offer on the mansion in Allendale. Denise had shown her that living in opulence didn't bring happiness. In fact, Amy loved puttering around in the little flower garden and moving the smaller furniture around to suit her moods. In the mansion, the furniture was much too heavy and cumbersome to change on a whim.

She tossed and turned most of the night, but eventually she found sleep. And she woke up fifteen minutes before the alarm clock was set to go off. Her excitement couldn't be contained, so she quit trying.

Amy jumped up, showered, fluffed her hair, and carefully applied her makeup. She ate an English muffin with marmalade, not stopping to savor the flavor like she normally would. She couldn't. Today was the first day of her new life. She was to embark on a journey that would lead her to establishing herself as an adult.

With car keys in hand, Amy flung her purse over

her shoulder, and headed for the door. It sure did feel nice to have the freedom of mobility that being able to drive brought. This was another thing she owed Denise, who'd taken a huge risk and encouraged her to get her driver's license.

Clearview was a small town, so it only took a few minutes to get to the temp agency. Carol was waiting at the front desk for her with a huge grin plastered across her face.

"You're gonna like what I've got lined up for you, Amy. C'mon back to my office."

Amy sat down across from Carol and listened as the owner of the agency explained where she was going and what she was supposed to do. "Every year, there's an antique car show in Plattsville. Dealers and car enthusiasts come from all fifty states to look and buy. Most of the dealers bring their own staff and models, but a few of them run on lean budgets, so they hire people to man the booths."

"I'll be selling cars?" Amy asked, her heart falling. She knew very little about cars. How was she supposed to sell them?

"Well, in a way, I guess," Carol replied as she stood up and came around from behind her huge oak desk. "But all you really have to do is smile, look good, and act like you're having a good time. You'll be more like a hostess rather than a car salesperson."

Amy took the slip of paper with the job description from Carol. The job title was "Model," which gave her a little flutter of excitement. She'd never envisioned herself a model, other than for the charity events she'd been in at her daddy's country club. Back when she was a debutante, she'd worn designer gowns and floated down a makeshift runway so all the elderly matrons could swoon and imagine themselves young again. This was more real.

"Are you sure I can do this?" Amy asked after Carol was finished explaining the job.

"I have no doubt, Amy. You're a beautiful woman with more social graces than anyone I know. Just be yourself."

Amy nodded. She'd heard this expression more than once lately. "Be yourself," Denise had said when she first went to the temp agency and met Carol. Andrew had given her the same advice. Their words gave her the confidence she needed to nod and accept the assignment.

She was due to report to the auto show in two hours, giving her plenty of time to drive to Plattsville and find her way to the coliseum. It would be nice to scope the place out before she started working.

Plattsville was about the same size as Clearview, so it wasn't hard to find where she needed to go. Since only the dealers were there, the parking lot was only about a third full, mostly with trailers attached to trucks. Most of the people probably didn't want to drive their antique cars; they pulled them. Amy didn't understand the rationale behind owning a car you didn't drive, but she saw that quite a few people did.

Once she went inside, she checked in with the person at the door. He pointed to a corner of the coliseum and said, "Go to the red convertible and let them know you're here. They'll give you more detailed instructions, since they're the ones who hired you."

Her nervousness returned. Everyone around her seemed to know what was going on. Everyone but her, that is. She started walking slowly toward the red convertible, but picked up her pace when she realized people were stopping what they were doing and staring at her. She felt like a fish out of water.

The man standing beside the red convertible glanced up at her, but kept waxing the side panel of the door. This car was obviously his pride and joy, if the way he treated it was any indication of his feelings. She had to admit, it was a beautiful car. In fact, it was the prettiest one on the floor.

Once she got to the booth, she just stood there and waited, assuming he'd stop and ask her what she wanted. But he didn't. He just kept right on waxing, moving the rag in a circular motion that threatened to hypnotize her.

After a few more minutes, he stopped, turned around, and their gazes locked. Amy pulled her bottom lip between her teeth. His eyes narrowed, making her even more nervous. They stared at each other for so long, Amy couldn't hear anything else.

This man was drop-dead gorgeous. At least in her mind he was—with his almost-too-long, dark brown hair and sky-blue eyes. He wore a baby blue T-shirt that looked like it was made just for him and jeans that hung low on his hips. The running shoes on his feet made it look like he was ready to leap across the floor, which made her lips quiver with the threat of a smile. If he went anywhere, he'd have to get past her first, since she was blocking his entrance to the rest of the coliseum.

"Yes?" he finally said.

Amy gulped. "I'm supposed to report here at eleven o'clock. I know I'm early, but I thought I might be able to help out with something."

He didn't say a word. He just looked at her.

"Here," she said after she felt like she'd waited long enough. "Here's my paper you're supposed to sign."

With a quick nod, he replied, "Just put it on the table. I'll look at it later." Then, he turned toward his car and went right back to waxing it, leaving Amy standing there feeling really stupid. So what if he looked really good in jeans? That didn't excuse him from being nice, did it?

Amy opened her mouth to get his attention, but he jerked up and dropped his rag before she had a chance to say another word. He motioned to the car and said, "Go ahead and get to work, then. I'll be back later." Then he turned and left. The hot-looking guy was gone.

She had absolutely no idea what to do next. Everyone in the coliseum was either waxing their cars, filling out paperwork, or standing around in one of the many huddles, talking to other car people.

She was definitely out of her element here. Surely,

Carol would understand if she wanted a change of assignments. This would be better for someone who knew something about cars.

The first thing Amy did was pick up the rag the man had been holding. Placing it on the side of the car, she began to make sweeping, circular motions like she'd seen him do. Until he came back, she'd help wax his car. At least she wouldn't feel so stupid if she had something constructive to do.

Every once in a while, she glanced up to see what was going on around her. After about fifteen minutes, she spotted a woman climbing into a blue Roadster, using the backseat for a step stool, and sitting atop the back of the car. A man with a camera began to snap pictures of her in different poses. She must be a model, Amy thought.

As soon as the camera man left, Amy left her booth and headed over to where the woman now stood, grinning and looking around the room, not focused on any particular thing.

"Excuse me," Amy said as she approached the woman. "I've been hired by a temp agency to model here, but I've never done this before."

The woman turned her smile toward Amy and extended her hand. "Hi, I'm Patty. I do this all the time. It's easy." She hopped back into the Roadster and resumed her pose. "See? This is all you have to do. Just smile and show off the car like you own it yourself. Make people want to look at it and ask questions."

Amy nodded. "Thanks, Patty. I think I can do that."

Could she really? She wasn't sure, but she was determined to try.

"Sure, any time. What's your name?"

"Amy."

"Great, Amy. I'm sure we'll be seeing lots of each other. This show can get pretty long, so maybe we can take breaks together."

Amy had never thought about what she'd do on break, so she felt grateful to have met someone. "Sounds good to me."

As soon as she got back to the red convertible, she decided to practice her modeling poses. She did exactly what she'd seen Patty do. She climbed over the seat and hoisted herself into a position on the back of the car, taking extra precautions with her skirt to keep it in place.

"Hey, whaddya think you're doing, lady?" the male voice boomed from behind her.

Amy quickly whipped her head around and found herself looking at the hot-looking guy in the baby blue T-shirt and blue jeans. She felt her face get hot as she slowly got out of the car. The man didn't look happy at all. Maybe she wasn't what he'd expected when he called for a model.

"What are you doing on my car?" he asked, this time taking a step closer, one hand on his hip, the other gesturing frantically.

"I—I'm practicing my poses," she stuttered, not daring to look him in the eye. This was definitely not working out. What made her think she could do something like this, anyway?

"Poses?" he asked in a cynical tone. He stopped moving toward her and was settling back on his heels, his hand holding his chin as he studied her a little more closely. "What kind of poses?"

At first, Amy had been embarrassed that she wasn't what he'd wanted, but now she found herself getting mad. She had the right to be, didn't she? The man had virtually ignored her when she first walked up, and now he was acting like she was committing a criminal act.

"Look, mister. I don't know what you expected, but I've never done anything like this before. I have no idea what you want or even why I'm here, so if you'll just sign my papers, I'll go back and tell Carol to send you another model."

"Model? I never hired a model," he said as he picked the paper up from the table. After looking at it for a moment, he nodded and smiled, his straight, white teeth finally showing through from beneath his dark brown mustache. "Oh, now I see what happened." He pointed to another red car two booths down. "You're supposed to be working for Mike."

"You're not Mike?" Amy hated the fact that her voice squeaked, but she couldn't help it. She'd missed her mark by two stalls.

"I've been Zachary Harper all my life." Was he laughing at her? Amy wanted to walk up to him and peel that smirk off his handsome face, but she didn't.

She just stood there and glanced back and forth between Mike and Zachary, feeling even more stupid than she'd felt a few minutes ago.

"I'm so sorry," Amy finally said after she got her senses back. "This is so embarrassing." She stepped forward and tried to take the paper from his hand. "I wish you'd said something when I first got here." Now that she thought about it, she realized he hadn't even read the papers when she'd first given them to him.

He pulled it away from her. "Wait a minute . . ." Then, he narrowed his eyes and studied the paper. "Amy Mitchell, huh?"

Slowly, she nodded as she let out a long breath. "If you'll let me have my reporting papers, I'll go see Mike. Please accept my apology."

With a chuckle, Zachary shook his head. "No apology necessary. I was wondering why you were here. The guy who generally helps me detail my cars is sick, so I figured he sent you instead. But why he'd send someone dressed like that, I couldn't figure out."

Amy stood there as Zachary's gaze raked over her, his eyes first traveling from head to toe, then back up again. She felt a burning sensation in the pit of her stomach, but she forced herself to turn away.

"Here's your paper, Amy," he said. "And you may call me Zach. As you can see, I'm really into cars, so I'm sorry that I didn't catch the error sooner."

Amy took the paper and turned her back on Zach, which was extremely difficult, considering the fact that she could almost feel his gaze boring a hole through her. She felt an odd mixture of pleasure at his appreciation and anger over the fact that he seemed to be mocking her. Didn't he know she wasn't some bimbo who didn't have a brain in her head?

Mike had been watching the whole thing, Amy realized, and when she handed him her paper, he took it and nodded. "I see you've met Zach."

"Yes," Amy said without a clue as to what else to say. Now she really felt stupid.

"Don't worry about him. He carries a chip on his shoulder because some woman jilted him a few years ago."

So that explained it. She could tell he liked the way she looked, but he'd only looked at her and given her the feeling she shouldn't even be there.

Mike gave Amy directions as to what he wanted her to do. Within an hour, he had her feeling very comfortable around his vintage red Mustang. Mike was a real sweetheart in a sort of grandfatherly way. Too bad Zach didn't have some of his kindness.

It was almost time to call it a day when Zach came over and chatted with Mike. Amy did her best to keep her distance, but it was hard when they both turned around, looked at her, then started chuckling, like she was the punch line of a joke.

Chapter Two

"What do you mean, you're not going back?" Andrew bellowed over the phone. "You have an obligation to the employment agency."

"I know, I know," Amy said as she rubbed the back of her neck. "I'll just call her first thing in the morning and tell her she needs to send someone else to the show."

"What if she can't do that?" Andrew asked. "What if there's no one else to send?"

"Oh, I'm sure she can find someone else. It's really an easy job. All someone has to do is sit on a car and talk to people."

"Then what's the problem?" Andrew asked. "I thought you liked talking to people. In fact, that's what you do best, now that you've been transformed."

16

Amy giggled. Ever since that slumber party where Denise and a bunch of the other women in Clearview had done a makeover on her, Andrew had referred to it as her "transformation."

"I just don't want to do it, that's all." Amy didn't want to go any further into it. She just didn't want to go back.

"Suit yourself," Andrew finally said. "But I wouldn't expect Carol to bend over backwards looking for another job for you."

Andrew was probably right, Amy thought. She knew she was bombing out on Carol. But how could she face Mike after the way he and Zachary made her feel like a fool?

She'd call Carol first thing in the morning. It was too late to call now. The agency's offices had been closed for a couple of hours.

Sleeping was impossible. Amy had showered and put on her most comfortable pajamas, thinking she needed a good night's sleep before explaining to Carol how she didn't think this was the right job for her. But that was out of the question. She was worried about what Carol would say.

Finally, she got up, after her second night of very little sleep. Two cups of coffee and another hour later, she picked up Carol's business card and dialed the agency number.

"Oh, good, Amy, I was just getting ready to call you. Mike phoned from the car show yesterday, and he thanked me for sending you to him."

"He thanked you?" Amy asked, stunned by this information. She wouldn't have thought he'd thank Carol.

"Yes, in fact, he said you were perfect for the job. I knew you'd do me proud."

Amy let out an audible sigh. This was *not* what she'd expected.

"Now, what can I do for you, Amy?"

She licked her lips, studied her manicure and forced herself to say, "I just called to let you know I found the booth without any problem. I'll be there at ten o'clock this morning as planned."

"You do realize there's overtime involved here, don't you?" Carol asked. "If you can't do it, I'm not sure who I'll send. We're already stretched pretty tight on personnel. All my reliable people have been placed."

Well, that answered that, Amy thought. "Of course, I'll be able to do it. What else do I have to do at night?"

Carol chuckled. "You're such an attractive young woman, Amy, I was worried you might have dates lined up every night of the week."

Flattery will get you anywhere. "No, that hasn't happened yet," Amy said. "I'll work the overtime."

"Let me know if something happens," Carol said right before they hung up.

Amy flopped back onto a chair, working hard at catching her breath. She'd expected to call Carol and possibly have to convince her she needed another assignment. She hadn't expected this.

Mike actually thanked Carol? Was he crazy, or what? Wasn't it obvious that she didn't belong in a car show, modeling something she knew absolutely nothing about? She didn't even understand half of what people were saying about the cars, once they went beyond the make, model, year, and color.

Amy's wardrobe now consisted of bright, cheerful dresses, suits, slacks, and blouses that she and Denise had picked out. She chose a pale yellow pair of linen slacks and a turquoise and yellow silk blouse. Then she topped it with the matching linen jacket that enhanced the color of her highlighted hair. She knew she looked good as she stepped outside the cottage.

All the way to Plattsville, Amy lectured herself. This was more of a stretch than she ever thought she'd have to make, but she didn't have any choice. People were counting on her; she had to do the responsible thing.

When she pulled into the parking lot, Amy noticed how it had begun to fill up. People milled around outside the coliseum door, waiting for the show to open so they could look at old cars. She'd been given a special pass that she wore on a string around her neck. The guard smiled as he opened the door and let her in.

Mike wasn't anywhere near his booth. Amy was actually glad about that, since she wanted to get into position before having to face him.

Patty walked by on her way to where she was modeling, and waved. "Wanna go to lunch on break?"

"Sure," Amy said. "What time?"

"I'll let you know in about an hour. We have to figure out when it's best for Mike and my boss."

Amy was glad to have something to look forward to and someone who'd done this before to ask questions. Patty was such a sweet woman, she had no doubt she could throw any question her way, and she'd get an honest answer.

To Amy's surprise, Mike and Zach walked up the aisle together about five minutes before the show was supposed to open. Mike nodded to Zach, and they parted ways, but not in the direction she would have expected. Rather than head straight for his own booth, Zach came up to her.

"Uh, Amy," Zach began, "I was wondering if you have plans for lunch."

Amy nodded, unable to find her voice. She opened her mouth, but quickly closed it with an apologetic smile.

"You do have plans, right?" He didn't bother to hide his disappointment. "Maybe some other time."

"Yes, maybe another time."

Zach started to leave, but he abruptly turned back to face her. "How about tonight? Are you staying until closing?"

Again, Amy nodded. "I'll be here through the entire show."

"Good," he said with a smile. "How about taking a break around six o'clock for dinner?"

"I'm not sure how many breaks I'll have."

"Trust me. Mike and I are old friends. He'll give you as many breaks as you need."

Amy slowly smiled back at him. "Okay, then I'll have dinner with you around six." Was she really accepting? Even as the words left her mouth, Amy couldn't believe what was happening.

"It's a date."

Her head felt light as she resumed her position beside the car. Amy felt as though she'd just awakened from a dream, although she knew it was for real. Zachary Harper had just asked her out to dinner, and although only yesterday she had wanted to run away and never come back, she was thrilled at the prospect of spending time with him. After all, he certainly did look good. If nothing else, she could gawk.

Amy's smile never left her face, and people responded by grinning back. It was a completely different experience for her, yet it was something she'd been trained to do as a child.

The blue blood in Amy's veins was the reason she knew all the right things to say and do, but in a social situation completely different from this. She looked around at all the jeans-clad young people and the country western band playing in the center of the coliseum, and she realized this was really the same thing, only with a different clientele. And she had to admit, this group seemed to be having a lot more fun than her parents' social crowd at the country club.

Men ogled cars, women got in and had their pictures taken behind the wheels of cars their grandparents probably drove, and children ran around chasing each other, squealing and drawing attention from everyone there. It was almost like a circus, only more fun for Amy because she'd met some new people.

The morning seemed to fly by. Before she knew it, Patty was standing beside her booth, pointing to her watch.

Amy glanced over at Mike, who was standing off to one side talking to a customer. He'd noticed Patty, though, and he nodded for her to go ahead.

"How'd it go?" Patty asked as they made their way to the snack bar. "Looks like you've been pretty busy."

"I've been so busy I lost track of time. I never had any idea so many people liked antique cars."

"My dad was an enthusiast, so I was raised in places like this."

"Your dad collects cars?" Amy asked.

Scrunching up her nose, Patty nodded. "Yes, but you won't believe what he collects."

"What?"

"Hearses." Patty made several faces, making Amy laugh. "I was embarrassed when he drove me to school because I always arrived in a hearse. Boys used to sing that old song 'Pray For the Dead.' I hated the hearses, but I have to admit I love old cars."

Amy couldn't imagine what it would have been like to arrive at school in a hearse. She'd always come by limo with her family's driver at the wheel. And she didn't remember a single time when her father took her to school.

"What do you drive?" Amy asked.

"I have several cars, but I have most of them in the shop. Right now I use an old pickup truck because I'm rebuilding the engine in my Corvair."

"You're rebuilding the engine?" Amy asked in amazement. "Yourself?"

Nodding, Patty chuckled. "I know it's hard to picture me doing that, but it's what I enjoy in my spare time. Most of my good memories are from my childhood when I used to spend all day Saturday with my father in the garage out behind the house."

Amy was definitely impressed. "I've never even looked under the hood of my car, let alone done work on it."

"Are you interested?" Patty asked.

With a shrug, Amy replied, "I'm not sure. I've never really thought about it before."

"You might want to consider doing a little auto maintenance. Even if you don't want to do it for a living or make it your hobby, you certainly can save a lot of money if you know how to change your own oil and do the tune-ups."

Amy decided not to tell Patty she never had to worry about money. It was obvious that she was in the minority.

48165

"I'll have to seriously consider it, then. It makes sense for a woman to know those things."

"Yes," Patty agreed. "It certainly does."

They talked about almost everything during lunch. Amy learned that Patty's dad had connections with all the antique auto dealers, so she stayed pretty busy working the shows. This was how she earned enough money to support her hobby. And once in a while, she was able to sell one of her cars for a hefty profit, which she said brought her more happiness than anything else.

"What do you know about Zach Harper?" Amy asked with a little hesitation.

Patty shrugged. "A little. What do you wanna know?"

"Is he nice?"

"He's okay. A little defensive, maybe."

Amy had noticed that. "I wonder why."

"Rumor has it he was jilted by his long-time girlfriend, and he doesn't want to get burned twice."

Now that made sense. No wonder he looked at her so cynically.

Patty arched a brow. "Interested in him romantically?"

The heat that rose to Amy's cheeks flustered her. She rarely blushed, but she knew her feelings were now obvious. No sense in denying the facts.

"Well, sort of."

"Just be careful. Everyone I know who thinks she has a chance with Zach gets hurt."

Amy didn't like what she was hearing, but she was glad Patty warned her. At least she knew to guard her heart.

"Thanks for the advice. I'll make sure I keep my distance."

Patty glanced at her watch. "We'd better get back to our stations. Those guys need us to sell their cars."

Mike was standing with the same person when Amy got back. She knew the man was interested in buying one of Mike's three cars on the display floor, which was good, since Mike had a couple more cars he wanted to bring into the arena. The problem was that there wasn't enough room to bring in more than three at a time.

"Hey, Amy, would you mind if I left for a few minutes?" Mike said. "I have to talk to the finance guys so we can finalize this deal."

"Sure, Mike. Anything new I need to know?"

He glanced over at his customer and nodded. "Yeah, the blue Rolls is sold, so you need to start talking up the pink Caddy I have out in the holding lot."

This part of her job was fun. Amy thoroughly enjoyed telling prospective customers about the cars Mike had shown her when he brought her outside the day before. And she remembered the pink Cadillac because of the Bruce Springsteen song. Hopefully, she'd get a chance to sit in it once it came inside the coliseum.

Amy spoke to everyone who stopped. Once, when she was chatting with an elderly couple, her peripheral vision picked up the fact that Zach was facing her, standing with his hands on his hips. When she turned to look squarely at him, she saw that he was staring directly at her with great interest. Patty was talking to him about something.

When he spotted her looking back, he lifted a hand and waved. She tentatively waved back, then returned her attention to the couple who'd been admiring the red Mustang. It was a classic car, she'd learned, and it was in great demand, which was why it had such a hefty price tag.

"I'm not really all that anxious to sell her," Mike had admitted. "She gets a lot of attention for my booth, so I use her to attract customers."

Amy could see the logic in that. But she still didn't think he should overvalue his car in the market. Like he said, though, who knew? Someone might want the car badly enough to pay what he was asking.

Mike was gone a couple of hours. He came back with a smile on his face.

"My customer qualified for the loan," he said. "Now we can bring in the Caddy right after dinner." Then, he snapped his fingers. "Which reminds me. Zach wants to take you out someplace nice. Is that all right with you?"

Chapter Three

Amy nodded. Of course it was all right with her. She'd already accepted the date, and she naturally assumed Mike knew that, so why was he asking her?

Her question was answered with his next comment. "I thought you and Zach might want to help me drive the Caddy inside before you go. I have a feeling you won't be coming back. Oh, and I need to let you know that I'm not paying you for your time after you leave here."

With a smile, Amy said, "I wouldn't expect you to. And yes to the other question. I certainly don't mind helping with the car, and Zach probably won't mind, either."

It surprised Amy when Zach grumbled at the special

request. "When was the last time you helped me out, Mike?"

Mike snickered. "When I hired Amy. If it weren't for me, you wouldn't have a date with such a pretty girl."

Amy smiled, in spite of the fact that they were talking about her like she didn't exist. It felt good to be noticed for something other than her pedigree.

"Okay," Zach said, sighing. "Since you're getting geriatric, I'll give you a hand. Wouldn't expect an old man to do something so strenuous."

Amy's head whipped around to get Mike's reaction. She didn't expect his hearty laughter.

"Just wait 'til you're my age, Zach. You'll see what it's like."

Actually, Mike wasn't old. In fact, Amy figured him to be slightly older than her own father. But he acted more like a grandfather than a dad. He was indulgent and jolly.

With the thinning crowd, it wasn't too hard to maneuver the Cadillac into the arena. And people moved to one side to let the car through, most likely because they were used to this. Amy wasn't. She was a nervous wreck as she acted as traffic director with Zach at the wheel.

Patty giggled with delight when she saw the pink car. "Wanna trade places?" she asked. "I've always wanted a car like this. It's so ostentatious."

With both eyebrows raised, Mike agreed. "That it is Patty, but I won't let Amy out of her job just because you happen to like pretty cars. She's been with me since the beginning of this show, and she gets the pleasure of showing it off."

"Lucky girl," Patty said with a fake pout. Then she turned to Amy, winked, and whispered, "I heard you have a date with Zach. Just remember to keep him guessing."

"Keep him guessing?" Amy had no idea what Patty meant by this comment.

"Yeah. He's hot looking, and he knows it. But he doesn't have to know how interested you are. Let him wonder. Be a woman of mystery." She paused for a second before adding, "And guard your heart."

Now she understood. It was all about their discussion at lunch in the snack bar. "I'll try my best," Amy said. "But I'm not used to playing games with men."

"You need to learn," Patty said. "Give me a call sometime, and I'll be glad to give you a few pointers."

Amy had no doubt Patty had plenty of suggestions and helpful hints as far as men were concerned. And she suspected they were all good ones, too. The problem was, she didn't really believe in playing games in relationships. She wanted something more solid and real, like what her brother Andrew had with Denise. Now that was an awesome relationship.

Once the Cadillac was positioned and parked, Zach turned to Amy and said, "Let me make sure my help knows how to close up shop, and we can get outta here."

Amy nodded. Mike was obviously right. Zach had no intention of returning to the show.

She knew the moment they left the arena that she needed to guard her heart. Zach was not only eye candy, he was charming, making her feel more special than any guy had ever made her feel. His appreciative glances gave her goosebumps, melting her reserve and taking her to a place she'd never visited with her emotions. But whenever he had the chance, he also let her know this was just a date, not a relationship in the making.

Denise had failed to tell her what to do at a time like this. Amy looked at Zach, forcing herself to remember what Patty had told her. He'd been jilted. He was jaded.

"Any place you'd like to go?"

Amy racked her brain. The only restaurant she knew about in Plattsville was the Pine Room. She shrugged. "I'm not sure. I've only been here a few times, and I ate at the Pine Room."

He studied her with an expression she couldn't read. "Did you like it?"

"Yes, it was very good."

"Then let's go there. I'm always in the mood for a good steak."

Amy had no idea what Zach's financial situation was, but she knew that the Pine Room was expensive. Traditionally, she knew it was his place to pay since he'd invited her, but she didn't want him to be strapped for cash. But her upbringing prevented her from directly asking him.

Zach had to unhitch the trailer from his pickup truck, which sat in a row among a sea of even more trucks. Amy had never ridden in a truck before, and she was excited.

He brushed his hands together when he was finished, then looked at Amy. "You're pretty when you smile."

Her face grew hot again. Blushing was something she'd been trained not to do, but she couldn't help it. Zach caused her to react in ways that were out of her control.

"Thank you, Zach," she said in a soft voice.

He opened the passenger door and offered her a hand to climb in. The cab of the truck was nothing like what she'd pictured. The seats were a soft leather that felt as smooth as silk. On the dashboard, she saw an electronic panel that showed more about the inner workings of the truck than she cared to know. He had a CD player as well as drink holders for two passengers. It was actually quite nice. Plush, even.

"Like my new truck?" he asked as he slid into the driver's side. "I just got it last week."

"Very nice." Amy rested her arm on a leather cushioned pad Zach had lowered between them. She couldn't help but notice the barrier. Was it for comfort or to keep her at a distance?

Zach started the engine and moved slowly toward the exit of the parking lot. Once they were on the road, he turned briefly to her. "Mike said you live in Clearview. I thought I knew everyone in town, but I don't remember hearing your name. How long you been there?"

"Not long," Amy said. "My family's from Nashville. When my brother got a job in Clearview, I wanted to go with him to see what the rest of the world is like."

Zach belted out a hearty laugh. "Clearview isn't exactly the rest of the world, Amy. You should have gone to New York for that. Or at least Los Angeles."

Amy smiled with her lips shut. She couldn't tell him that any place outside of Nashville was an adventure for her. Although her parents had loved her dearly, they were terribly overprotective. She had to get away, or she might never have discovered that she could take care of herself.

With his eyes focused on his driving, Zach continued talking. "I've lived on the outskirts of Clearview all my life. My parents still have twenty acres that my dad farms, but they've been selling off tracts as they get older."

"Farming sounds like a lot of fun," Amy said. And it did. She'd only read about farming, and she thought it would be a great way to grow up.

He shrugged. "I suppose it might be fun to some people, but it's also a lot of work."

"Yes, I suppose it is." Amy turned to face him. "Do you still live with your parents?"

"No, I moved out as soon as I turned twenty-one. I

went to the junior college in Plattsville and worked part-time for a friend at an auto repair shop, and when it was time to move to the University, I knew what I wanted to major in."

"What's that?"

"Industrial technology." He pulled into the Pine Room parking lot. "Well, here we are. Wait right here. I'll come around and help you out."

Amy thought about Zach's major as she sat waiting for Zach. Industrial technology? What was that?

Although Zach was guarded to a point, he was a pretty decent conversationalist. In fact, he gave her plenty of opportunities to ask questions, and he didn't seem to mind answering them, as long as she didn't dig too deep. He'd obviously mastered the fine art of avoidance. Talking about his job, his antique car hobby, and where he lived was okay. His family and anything personal about his past were off-limits. She didn't miss the pained expression on his face when she asked him if he'd ever been married.

"No," he replied. Then, after grimacing, he quickly changed the subject.

Zach couldn't believe he was sitting here in his favorite restaurant of all time with a gorgeous woman who obviously came from the upper class. He'd sworn off women after Melody had broken off their engagement. Putting himself back in the position of letting another woman into his heart wasn't a good idea, but he was curious about Amy.

She was beautiful, and she had an air of self-confidence that came through the first time he laid eyes on her. Her speech was trained and cautious, but he sensed a warm, kind woman beneath that perfectly finished exterior. She seemed to have a zest for life, for the simple things he'd always taken for granted.

"Do you like steak?" he asked as the waiter left menus. "They also have excellent seafood."

"Either is fine with me," she replied.

Zach noticed how uncomfortable she looked. Amy wasn't out of her element in this posh restaurant, so what could be the problem?

"Are you sure you want to be here?"

Her eyes locked with his, and she slowly nodded. "I really like this place. But I don't know what I want. It all looks good." She hadn't even opened the menu, so he knew there was something else.

"How about a combination of steak and seafood?"

She continued looking at him, almost as if she was searching for something. "That would be fine," she said.

"Okay, then I'll order steak and seafood for both of us. Would you like wine?"

She shook her head. "No thanks. I have to drive home, and wine makes me sleepy."

"Good move," he said with a nod. He wasn't much of a drinker, so he was relieved that she wasn't either. "How about iced tea?"

Amy flashed that million-dollar smile and nodded. "Yes, that sounds good."

All the way to the Pine Room, conversation had flowed very smoothly. He'd had to deflect a few personal questions, but they managed to get right back on track to things he didn't mind discussing. What was going on now? he wondered. Suddenly the conversation seemed stilted.

"So, Amy, how long have you been into modeling?" he asked, figuring he was now in safe territory. Focusing on her rather than him would make it much easier to keep the conversation flowing without making him uncomfortable.

"This is my first modeling job," she replied without hesitation.

"You're kidding."

"No." She shook her head. "I would have thought it was obvious by now, especially after yesterday when I sat on your car."

Zach chuckled. He had to admit, he didn't like anyone touching his cars, but when he'd gotten close enough to get a good look at Amy, some of the anger faded. She looked mighty good sitting on his car. If he hadn't already made such an issue of not wanting to hire models to help him at shows, he probably would have made her a better offer on the spot.

"That's the kind of mistake anyone could have made, even with experience. I find it hard to believe you've never done modeling before. It looks like second nature to you."

"Afraid not," Amy said with a puzzled expression. He sure did wish he knew what was on her mind.

"Modeling is a lot more difficult than I ever imagined it would be."

"Why's that?"

"Well," she began, looking around the room, then quickly back at him, catching him staring at her. "First of all, it's hard to hold a smile for so long when you don't have anything to smile about."

"I'm sure you have plenty to smile about, Amy."

She grinned back at him. His chest thudded. "Yes, I suppose I do. I have a nice home, good parents, a brother who looks after me, a very sweet sister-in-law, and some nice friends."

"What? No steady guy?" Why did he have to ask such a stupid question? Besides, what did it matter? He sure didn't want anything from her.

Amy shook her head. "No, not yet, anyway."

"I'm surprised some man hasn't swept you off your feet, Amy," Zach said, trying hard to sound like a big brother, but not feeling that way at all. "You're very attractive and from what I can tell, smart and fun to be around."

Her eyes lit up. "You really think so? I mean do you think I'm fun?" Was that hope he heard in her voice?

"Yes, Amy, I think you're fun." *Too much fun.* Zach wished he'd kept his distance. He was getting in way over where he wanted to be with Amy Mitchell. She was much too desirable for him to take a chance. He'd lost his heart once, and now it needed guarding.

Amy let out a sigh, propped her elbows on the table, and clasped her hands beneath her chin. There was a twinkle in her eye that hadn't been there before. Was it possible he was responsible for it?

Chapter Four

"**W**hat do you mean, you went off with some guy?" Andrew bellowed over the phone. "How do you know he's not some serial killer or something?"

"Oh, come on, Andy. I know better than to go off with someone who seems suspicious."

"How do you know for sure?" he asked, sounding just like their father.

She cleared her throat. "Andrew, you're going to have to stop treating me like a child. I'm a grown woman, and I know what I'm doing."

Amy heard Andrew cup the mouthpiece of the receiver and some muffled voices in the background. Obviously, he was conferring with Denise, who was almost always on Amy's side during one of these disagreements.

"Okay, Amy," he finally said after almost a whole minute. "You're a big girl now, so I guess I can trust you to make decisions without me."

"No, Andrew," Amy said with the authority of a schoolteacher. "I'm not a big *girl*. I'm a grown *woman*." She giggled. "Repeat after me. Amy Mitchell is a grown woman."

"C'mon, Amy. This is silly."

"No, Andrew. I want to hear you say it. Amy Mitchell is a grown woman."

He let out a breath. "Amy Mitchell is a grown woman."

He said the last two words so fast they ran together. It was tempting to make him say it again, but that might be pushing it.

"Okay, that's better."

"Do you have plans to see him again?"

"Why, yes, as a matter of fact, I'll be seeing him first thing in the morning."

"Isn't this a little fast?"

As irritating as he was, Amy still found her brother to be a sweet pest. "I'm working two booths down from him all day and into the night. We'll be seeing a lot of each other for the next few days."

"Oh, yeah, that's right."

"Don't worry so much, Andy. I really do know what I'm doing."

"I s'pose you do." Andrew paused for a moment before saying, "So you really like this guy?"

"I'm not sure yet, but you'll be among the first to know when I figure it out."

"Please, please be careful."

"Okay. Lemme talk to Denise. Love you." She made a smacking sound into the receiver to emulate a kiss.

"Hi, there, Amster. What's shakin'?" Denise's voice was always upbeat and fun to hear. "See any hot-looking guys at the car show?"

"Yeah, I saw a bunch of 'em." Amy giggled. "I even went out to dinner with one."

"Holy cow, Amy! You don't mess around, do you? That's fast work, even for me. How'd you do it?"

"I sat on his car when I first got there. He asked me what I was doing, and he told me to get off his car."

"Well, that's the most unusual pick-up line I've ever heard, but if it works for you, who am I to say anything?"

Amy laughed out loud. "We went to the Pine Room."

"Oh, wow! He's a big spender, on top of everything else. You better snag this one before someone else discovers him."

"I don't think he's in the market to get snagged. But I'm having a good time. This temp job is really fun, Denise."

"I thought you'd enjoy working different jobs. That's how I knew what I wanted."

"But there weren't any bookstores in Clearview.

How did you know you wanted to own that kind of business?"

"I've always loved to read books, and I knew I wanted to have my own business after working for so many different entrepreneurs. I knew it would be a good fit."

"The only thing I know how to do now is hop up on the backseat of a convertible, pose, wave, and smile."

"That's a start." Denise laughed as she spoke, so Amy laughed right along with her. It felt good to be lighthearted with her sister-in-law. Denise was a wonderful balance for Andrew's serious nature. "You'll pick up a few things from each job, so relax and enjoy it."

"I hope it's all stuff I can use."

"Keep us posted on how things go with this guy, Amy. Oh, and the job, too. Call and give us an update."

When Amy hung up, she was smiling, something Denise never failed to make her do. She felt blessed to have such a wonderful family, but she also knew that the smothering love of her parents had held her back from developing into the person she was becoming. They loved her too much, and now it was up to her to assert her independence.

By the time she lay down in her bed, Amy was so sleepy from a busy day and two sleepless nights, she was out like a light before any new thoughts formulated in her mind. And she didn't awaken until her clock sounded in the morning.

Fortunately, all she had to do was switch on the coffee she'd prepared the night before, hop in and out of the shower, put her makeup on that she was getting used to wearing, and pull on the lavender skirt and sweater set she'd picked out and hung on her closet door before she went to sleep. Amy had always been very organized. She was glad she finally had a reason to be.

When she arrived at the coliseum in Plattsville, there weren't as many cars in the lot as there had been the day before. But she knew the largest crowds generally arrived in the afternoon and evening.

Mike's appreciative gaze made her feel good. Amy knew all her clothes were tastefully stylish because Denise had helped her pick them out. At first, she'd resisted on a few of them, thinking her parents would never approve of her wearing the short skirts that showed her entire knee and even a couple inches of her thigh. But Denise reminded her that all her vital parts were still covered, and this still wasn't as short as some people wore them.

"You better stay away from Zach today, Amy," Mike said when she got close enough to hear him.

"Why?" Had something happened?

His whole face broke into a smile. "He won't get any work done if he takes a good look at you."

Amy grinned back at his compliment. Mike was

mostly all business, but once in a while he made a comment that made her feel special.

Patty ran by and waved with one hand while she tried to button her jacket with the other. She was running late as usual, and the building was cold, since not as many people were in there to heat up the place.

The smaller crowd actually produced more sales results for all the dealers. With fewer people on the floor, the customers were able to get better service from the dealers and hired help, so they were able to make more informed decisions. One thing Amy had learned in the short time of being around these people was that most of them were very smart, and nearly all of them were passionate about old cars.

"They certainly don't build 'em like they used to," was one phrase she'd heard over and over throughout the day.

Her response was always, "No, they sure don't. May I help you with something?"

Mike had given her a price sheet and a little information about the cars he had in his shop, as well as the ones he had at the show. "If all these cars sell, I'll just bring in more from my place," he told her.

Good. Amy was concerned that he'd sell all his cars, and she'd be out of a job before the week was over. She was glad she hadn't decided not to come back after her first embarrassing encounter with Zach.

She didn't see Zach all morning, with the exception of the times she spotted the back of his head as he spoke with a couple of his customers. Mike had told her that Zach was one of the best in the business and that there was no doubt he had the best cars mechanically of anyone in the room.

"Zach is the only guy I know who knows the old Chevy engines inside and out," he said. "And he can spot a problem with any make of car."

Amy wasn't sure what it was, but she was beginning to enjoy all aspects of this business. She appreciated the fact that these cars were built many years before she was born, yet they were all still in excellent condition. There wasn't a single car in the arena that had a dented fender or torn upholstery.

"This is a juried show," Mike had explained. "They have to approve of not only the dealers but the cars. I had to send them a picture of all my cars that I'd even consider putting on the floor. And I signed a statement agreeing to back up anything that went out of here. That's why we can ask top dollar for these antiques."

Patty was another person Amy enjoyed chatting with. They had lunch again.

"Can you believe that royal blue Jaguar sold for the asking price?" Patty said. "It's a gorgeous car, but I never dreamed Hank would get the kind of money he was asking."

For the first time, Amy actually understood. She nodded, feeling pretty smug about her new knowledge. "I know, but some people will pay anything to get whatever it is they want."

Patty tilted her head to one side and studied Amy.

"Sounds like you might have some experience with this. I don't know much about you, Amy. What are you hiding from the world?"

Amy let out a loud snicker. "Hiding? I'm not hiding anything."

"But we don't know much about you. What did you do before you got this job with the temp agency?"

"Not much. I worked in a bookstore for a few months."

Patty crinkled her nose. "Sounds pretty boring. I don't think I could do that."

"Actually, I enjoyed it. The job was anything but boring."

"What's there to do at a bookstore?"

Amy thought for a moment before replying. "First of all, I sold books. Some people came in knowing what they wanted, but others only had a vague idea. I enjoyed helping them figure out what to buy. And we had story hour for children. I read stories and did puppet shows while their moms shopped."

"Ugh!" Patty said, her nose still crinkled. "I still can't imagine. Give me a wrench and an engine, and I can show you a really good time."

Patty's outlook was different from Amy's, but Amy really enjoyed being around someone so different. She'd never known anyone quite like Patty before, especially not a woman who knew her way around a car engine.

"Can you actually fix everything in a car?" Amy asked before taking another bite of her sandwich.

Nodding, Patty replied, "Almost everything. These days cars are computerized, so there's very little guesswork. I enjoy working on the old cars, taking them apart, looking everything over, diagnosing the problem. It's like a jigsaw puzzle in 3-D."

"I never thought about it like that, but I can see what you're saying."

"But I think for the average consumer, newer cars are the best. When something breaks down, all we have to do is hook it up to a computer, and the problem shows up on the screen in a matter of minutes. Sure does save a lot of time and money."

That was why Amy figured she'd always have a new car. Now that she had the mobility of her own wheels, she couldn't imagine being without them while they were being worked on.

"Why, Amy?" Patty asked. "Thinking about becoming a mechanic?"

That had been the last thing Amy saw herself doing, but she didn't laugh. In fact, she thought she might even consider it. Wouldn't Andrew have a fit if he knew what was going on in her mind now? And her dad would never speak to her again!

Patty leaned forward and whispered, "Don't look now, but I think we're about to have company."

Acting on instincts rather than doing what she was told, Amy quickly turned around to see who was coming. Her heart leapt when she saw that it was Zach. He smiled at her, then nodded toward Patty.

"I think that's my cue to leave now," Patty said. She was gone before Amy had a chance to stop her.

"Didn't mean to run her off," Zach said without looking like he meant it.

"I don't think you ran her off. She had an appointment with a guy who wanted more information on the car she's been working on."

Zach chuckled. "Patty is definitely a different breed. She's a knockout, but she's a highly skilled mechanic. I'd trust her to work on my car any time."

"Really?" Amy said. She'd heard almost the exact same comment about Zach. "Most guys wouldn't want a woman to work on their car."

He shrugged. "I guess you're probably right, but anyone who knows Patty knows that she's good with an engine. I imagine it took her a lot of time and hard work to gain the reputation she has now."

Amy laughed. "Now I feel stupid."

"Why's that?" Zach leaned forward, enabling her to smell his aftershave, shampoo, and soap, their scents intermingling and creating his own special smell.

"When I first met Patty, I assumed she was just a model."

"I can see where you'd get that idea."

"Her fingernails aren't even dirty." The instant that came out of Amy's mouth, she was embarrassed. It sounded pretty stupid and petty for her to have noticed.

Zach burst out laughing. He held his hands out for her inspection and said, "My nails aren't dirty, either."

No, they weren't. In fact, his hands were spotless, but she could see the calluses from hard manual work.

"It's amazing what a good manicure can do for a mechanic," Zach continued. "And Patty told a bunch of us once that she always has acrylic nails applied for these shows because it's easier to show a car if she can use her hands and not feel embarrassed about it."

Amy saw how Zach looked down at her hands that were both resting on the table. She'd gone for a weekly manicure ever since her makeover. The Cut 'n Curl was a full service beauty salon, and she'd used the services of everyone there, from the top hairdresser to the makeup artist, all the way to the manicurist. It was fun to be pampered.

"You have pretty hands," Zach said softly. He reached out to take one of them, wrapping his large fingers around her tiny wrists. "And so small, too." He quickly let go, almost as if she'd burned him with her touch.

"I have long fingers," she said. Amy had to fight the urge to reach out and grab Zach's hand again. She wanted him to touch her and to feel that tingling sensation she'd felt just a few seconds earlier.

"So you do," he said, still looking at her hands. "I bet you play the piano."

"Yes." All women of her breeding had taken piano lessons. They'd even had the same teacher who came to their houses, making the rounds on Tuesday and Thursday afternoons after school.

"Would you consider playing for me sometime?"

* * *

The way Amy looked at Zach when he said that sent his heart diving directly to his stomach. A combination of shock and pleasure showed on her face. What had he gotten himself into?

"I'd love to," she replied softly. "Do you have a piano?"

Zach shook his head. "Not now. I used to play a little when I was a kid. My parents figured it would keep me out of trouble to learn to play a musical instrument, but I lost interest when I discovered sports."

Amy's laughter sounded like music. "Most guys would rather be on a sports field than cooped up in a parlor on a pretty day."

"Parlor? Sounds like something only the very rich would have in their houses."

He watched Amy's face as it suddenly took on a look of panic. What had he said to bring on such a reaction?

"Are you okay, Amy?"

"Y-yes, I'm fine," she stuttered.

Zach knew he had to say something to change her mood back to where it was. "Do you play sports?"

"I've always wanted to, but my parents were afraid I'd get hurt. I learned to ride horses, but they insisted on English style, and I wanted to ride Western."

Yes, now it was obvious that she came from money. Only women who came from very wealthy families rode English. But he couldn't mention money because it seemed to upset her when he did.

"I can't say I blame you, Amy. I've heard it's hard to keep your balance riding English."

"Exactly," she replied, her gaze holding his for several seconds. Clearly, there was some deep meaning behind that simple one-word expression. He had fought his feelings, but now he was determined to find out what made Amy Mitchell tick.

Chapter Five

If he only knew how powerful that comment was, Amy thought. Keeping her balance was something Amy had never been able to do with anything in her life until she'd learned to live on her own. And now that she had that balance, Zach was in her life, threatening to make her lose it.

It would have been different if they'd met through mutual friends, and he didn't have the emotional baggage of a past relationship that went sour. But she could tell he wasn't about to lose his heart to anyone.

Whenever they were on "safe" ground, he was open and free with information. However, the instant conversation turned to him and anything about his life, Zach clammed up. Amy didn't want to have to deal with that.

The problem she had was her attraction to him. At first, it was based on the way he looked, but now that she knew him a little better, she found that she really enjoyed being around him. He had a great sense of humor, and he was dedicated to his business. Amy had great respect for anyone who spent time working toward goals, and he was certainly goal-oriented.

He might be a mechanic, she thought, but he was among the very best, according to Mike. And that put him up on the top notch for her. Too bad he wasn't willing to open up about his personal life.

Then, Amy realized she was guilty of doing the same thing. Whenever anyone mentioned wealth or money, she felt a tightness in her chest. Now she knew she was ashamed having come from a rich family.

Her father's money had nothing to do with her, but other people perceived it differently. They automatically assumed she was helpless and needed her father's support to get by in life. That was why she hated telling anyone where she used to live in Nashville. It was common knowledge all over the South that the area was filled with old money and vast wealth.

"How's business?" Amy asked Zach after several minutes of silence.

"Couldn't be better," he replied. She could tell he'd been thinking, and she'd interrupted him.

"I'm surprised at how good business is for Mike, considering how few customers there are today."

"It's typical to have a huge turnout the first day of

the show, but most of those people are just lookers. The serious customers keep coming back."

Amy nodded. She'd seen many of the same people today that she'd seen yesterday. Mike had already answered quite a few questions, and he was anticipating having to bring in more cars before the end of the week.

"This is one of those things you never know until it happens," Zach continued. "I had one guy yesterday who told me he'd be here first thing this morning. He didn't show up, but I wasn't sure, so I turned away several prospects for the car he was looking at."

"It wasn't the red convertible, was it?" Amy asked, daring to look directly into his eyes.

A grin slowly widened his lips, and he shook his head. "No, Amy, it wasn't the car you tried to claim when you first got here."

She smiled back. He was teasing her, making her cheeks heat up again. "I'm surprised it hasn't sold yet, Zach. Seems like red convertibles are moving pretty fast."

"Why? Has Mike sold the Mustang?"

"No, but it's not because he hasn't had offers."

"He's got that thing priced way too high."

Shaking her curls, Amy replied, "If he wanted to sell it, he could. And he'd even make a nice profit if he sold it for our last offer."

Zach narrowed his eyes and looked at her quizzically. "You're really feeling like part of the show now, aren't you?"

"Yes, but why did you say that?"

"You said the word 'our.' That's a pretty telltale sign right there."

Amy laughed. "Yeah, I suppose it is. Mike has a way of making me feel important."

"According to him, you are. He says you're a natural with crowds like we've had."

"He told you that?" Amy asked. "What else did he say?"

"He thinks I should ask you out again."

That comment blind-sided Amy. She opened her mouth, but all that came out was a squeak.

Zach chuckled. "You don't have to go out with me if you don't want to."

"I-it's not that. It's just that I figured if you wanted to ask me out, you wouldn't need Mike to tell you to do it."

"I don't need him to tell me to ask you out, but it helps to have someone who agrees with me."

"Agrees with you?" Amy was confused as well as thoroughly flustered.

"Yes," Zach said, looking her directly in the eye. "He agrees that you and I need to get to know each other better."

Where did that come from? Zach wondered. Yes, Mike had told him he needed to get to know Amy better, but Zach had argued with him. He didn't need a woman in his life right now. All they did was complicate things.

Sitting here talking to Amy had turned him inside out. He was fascinated by her life. She was beautiful and open, yet mysterious in a way he couldn't describe. And he was dying to know more.

"So whaddya say, Amy? Would you like to go out again?" Zach found himself holding his breath, waiting for her answer. It suddenly meant a lot to him.

Her hesitation alarmed him. When she finally spoke up and said, "Yes, I'd like that," he thought he'd hit the moon, he was so happy.

"Good. This is a busy week until late Friday night, but I was thinking maybe after we wrap things up on Saturday I could follow you home and we could go somewhere in Clearview."

"Do you live in Clearview?" Amy asked.

"No, but it's not that far from where I live. My apartment is on the other side of Plattsville."

"Then it doesn't make sense for you to follow me home. We can leave from here, and you can bring me back to my car." She paused for a few seconds, then said, "Or I can drive. That way you won't have to pull the trailer off your truck."

Zach thought for a moment before nodding. When Amy offered to drive, he could tell she really wanted to. He had no idea why, but he certainly didn't mind being chauffeured around by a woman. Besides, it would give him a chance to study her face up close, something he'd been wanting to do since he'd first met her. If her attention was on driving, he could look to his heart's content without having her look back at him.

Patty winked as Amy walked by her booth to re-sume her post beside the car. Today, people seemed to want to take pictures, and it was her job to pose. Mike said it was nice to have the human touch in the pictures so people could look at them later and imag-ine themselves driving one of these vintage automo-biles. "Kind of like what they do in television commercials. The actors make the products look good."

Keeping that in mind, Amy pulled out all her smiles and looks of glee to make the cars look their very best. And Mike praised her for that. He actually told her he was going to request her for future jobs. "That is, if you don't mind," he added.

"No, of course I don't mind. I'm flattered."

Amy was now very comfortable with Mike, after spending so many hours by his side for three days. He really did remind her of a model grandfather. She saw his business ethics, which impressed her. There were many opportunities for him to lie in his own favor, but he never succumbed to temptation. He told the truth, whether it meant closing the deal or losing the prospect.

From the looks of things, most of the dealers here were honest, quite unlike the reputation of most car dealers. Either the antique car business was different, or the public's perception was off.

Amy got to know Patty pretty well during the week, between taking fifteen-minute breaks and having lunch together. It was fun to listen to someone who was passionate about her work. Patty had more energy than most of the people Amy knew back home, all put together. She wanted to remain friends with her after the show, and she told Patty.

"Yes, I'd like that, too," Patty said. "I don't have a lot of girlfriends because they think I'm weird for loving to tinker with cars. Sometimes I wish I could be more like them."

"Don't ever wish that, Patty. You're fine just the way you are."

With a shrug, Patty went on. "When I was a kid, I was more the type to climb trees and play ball than to play with dolls and things most girls liked. But I had brothers, and they didn't know much about what girls should do. I guess that's why I'm not as feminine as I should be."

"Oh, Patty, yes you are. Just because you like working on cars doesn't mean you're not feminine." Amy hated that Patty had been subjected to such meanness from people. If other girls and women would give Patty a chance, Amy had no doubt they'd find her just as fascinating as she did.

"Thanks, Amy. You're a sweetie. Maybe you can show me how to be a little more like a girl, and I can give you some pointers on how to save money on auto repairs." She thought for a second before adding, "Or better yet, I can do the repairs for you just for the cost of the parts."

That was the sweetest thing anyone had ever offered Amy. Patty had no idea about her family's wealth, and she was offering to help her save money. It almost brought tears to Amy's eyes. But she bit her bottom lip and nodded. "That would be wonderful. We'd better get back to work before they come looking for us."

Throughout the rest of the afternoon, Amy imagined what it would be like to have been a tomboy as a child. Patty was drop-dead gorgeous, but she didn't seem to realize it. She wore her makeup like the model she was, and she had a great figure. The tomboy she was telling Amy about was definitely hidden beneath the cute, form-fitting clothes she wore to the show.

Zach stopped by her booth and chatted with Mike a few times that afternoon. Once, when they didn't realize she was watching, they both turned around and looked at her. It was obvious they'd been talking about her, the way they both looked at the same time. She wasn't sure how to act after that.

Mike came up to her about an hour before the show was scheduled to be over that day. "Things have really slowed down, so you're free to go home if you'd like to."

Amy was awfully tired. She could use an extra hour of rest. "Are you sure?"

"Positive." He took a step back, turned toward Zach's booth, and crooked his finger. When Zach got close enough to hear him, Mike said, "Walk Amy to her car. I'll keep an eye on things for you."

Without a second's hesitation, Zach took Amy's hand and pulled her toward the exit. "I'm glad you had the sense not to go out there by yourself at this time of night."

Amy started to tell him she wasn't the one who thought of asking for his services, but she clamped her mouth shut. There wasn't any reason to tell him that. It would be okay for him to think she wanted him to walk with her.

"Nice night, isn't it?" he asked as soon as they stepped outside.

All the stars were out against the jet-black sky, reminding her of all the romantic movies she'd seen where the hero and heroine were taking a stroll in the privacy of darkness. She had to force herself to remember that this wasn't a romantic movie. In fact, it wasn't a romantic anything. Zach was doing her boss a favor and making sure she got to her car safely.

"Thanks, Zach," she said as they reached her car.

"Keys?" He reached out to take the keys she'd pulled from her purse.

She handed them to him. "I've really enjoyed working this week, even though the hours are a lot longer than what I'm used to."

"Pretty tiring, huh?"

"Very. But the work is so much fun, I'm able to forget about my tired feet until I get home. Then, I crash."

"Me, too."

Zach had handed her keys back to her, but he hadn't made a move to go back inside. He just stood there, holding her car door open, looking down at her. She could have sat there looking at him all night. The dim light from the moon, the stars and the streetlight highlighted his gold-streaked brown hair. His strong jaw looked more chiseled because of the night shadows.

If she didn't watch out, she knew she was in jeopardy of falling for Zach. But that wouldn't be smart because he didn't want a relationship. Their date on Saturday would probably be their last; at least, that's what she told herself. After that, she'd have to start thinking about her next temp job. Hopefully, she'd find something that would lead her to a business she was interested in. That was the point of this whole adventure, wasn't it?

All the way home, Amy's thoughts skitted from her busy day at the auto show, to Zach and his lean athletic build, to her future and what it might have in store for her, then back to Zach and the way it felt when his hand brushed hers. *Stop it!* Thinking about someone who might not even be interested was definitely something that could get her into trouble. She had to remain centered on her mission.

In spite of her exhaustion, Amy couldn't go to sleep right away. She was getting used to this, but she also knew she couldn't go around without any sleep. Instead of lying in bed, staring at the ceiling, Amy got up and fixed herself some hot milk.

That helped a little. She went back to bed with a magazine and read until her eyelids drooped shut. Then, she dreamed.

When the alarm clock went off, Amy sat up and almost fell out of bed. She was disoriented. Getting by with only a few hours of sleep each night was starting to catch up with her.

Today, she wore her turquoise jumpsuit. Mike grinned and nodded, giving her the thumbs-up sign. "Lookin' good, Amy," he said. "But then you always do. I'm glad Carol sent you."

It was strange to Amy to be valued mostly for the way she looked. But she knew Mike appreciated her people skills as well. He'd commented several times on how confident he was in her. "I don't have to tell you to go talk to a customer. You seem to know what to do on your own."

Amy smiled. She hadn't been head of the social committee of her debutante group for nothing. Being nice to people was what she did best.

Denise had recognized Amy's shyness in a new town for what it was: not knowing her way around and feeling out of place. Once her sister-in-law introduced her to the group she now called her friends, she was content, and her calendar was filled with all kinds of social engagements. This was a different kind of group from what she was used to, but she actually liked it better. People liked her for who she was rather than her family.

The parking lot had about the same number of cars

in it today as yesterday. Mike was right. The largest numbers came on the first day, and only serious buyers and lookers came back.

She was a little early, but she figured she'd go ahead and go inside. The snack bar was open, so she'd grab a cup of coffee before she went on duty.

"Hey, Amy," came a familiar voice from behind.

Amy whipped around to see Patty running to catch up with her. "You look happy about something."

Patty nodded. "I just sold one of my own cars I've been working on for nearly a year."

"Antique car?"

"Yep. And I got top dollar for it. I had that car in prime condition, so I was planning to hold out until I got what I was asking. It's kind of a shock that the right person came along yesterday and actually requested that particular model."

Patty had told Amy that she was allowed to discuss her own cars and business with the customers as long as she didn't pull people away from the show. Amy had no doubt Patty honored that, since she seemed to be an honest person.

"Well, congratulations, girlfriend," Amy said, imitating some of her new friends in Clearview. "Now what? Can you retire?"

The spark in Patty's eyes said it all. She was going to be able to do something soon, and she was anxious to share the news.

"Not retire, but now I can start looking for a location for my restoration shop."

Patty had shared her dream with Amy, which was to restore vintage cars and have a nationwide referral service for other antique auto buffs. It sounded interesting to Amy, especially since she'd only recently developed an interest in cars.

"Where are you going to look?"

With a shrug, Patty replied, "Plattsville, Clearview, and maybe even some of the other small towns around here. It'll have to be very inexpensive, though. I don't want to use all my profit from the sale."

"Must have been a mighty lucrative deal," Amy said.

"It was."

When they got inside, the first thing Amy did was glance over and look for Zach. She didn't think anyone saw her, but she was wrong.

"Zach's not here yet," Patty told her. "He has to pick up another car to replace the one he sold last night."

"Oh," Amy said, nodding, wishing she could have been more discreet about looking.

Patty glanced at her watch. "I think he'll be back around eleven this morning. I can't wait to see what he brings."

Amy needed to change the subject. Talking about Zach unnerved her, and she couldn't control the heat that kept rising to her face.

"What do you think you'll call your new business?" Amy asked.

"I haven't decided yet. I've thought about all sorts

of names, but nothing really hits me. I might want to figure out where I'm gonna be and whether or not I'll need a partner before I decide."

"Why would you need a partner?"

"Working on the engines and bodies of the cars is fun to me, but I don't really like having to deal with the interiors. I need a detail person and probably a business-minded person if I can find the combination."

"Is this business lucrative enough for you to have a partner?"

"It can be if I'm really careful what cars I buy. I'll also fix other people's cars, and I'll have to be the very best in order to keep my prices up."

Amy smiled at Patty and touched her shoulder. "I have a feeling you'll be the best in the country. People will line up for your services."

"Thanks, Amy," Patty said. "You're the only woman I know who seems to understand."

That comment meant a lot to Amy. She went inside, grabbed a cup of coffee, and headed for her booth where Mike was waiting for her.

"Patty's a good egg, isn't she?" Mike asked. He nodded toward where Patty was standing. "I saw the two of you talking."

"She's a very nice woman. I have a feeling she's going to go a long way in this business."

"Me, too," he said. "Her only problem is that she'd give away the farm on a deal. I'm surprised she got what she did for that old Ford."

"You know about her deal last night?"

"Of course I do. Everyone's talking about it."

Customers began to come inside, and they had to turn their attention to what they were there for. Amy kept glancing over at Patty and thinking how nice it would be to know exactly what she wanted to do and now have the means to go for it. Amy had the means but not the idea or the inclination. That was frustrating.

The noise in the coliseum was a steady roar until about a half hour before her lunch. Suddenly, it grew quiet, and all heads turned to the opening where dealers drove their cars through. She glanced up and saw the shiniest, the longest, and the prettiest car she'd ever seen in her life.

And Zach was behind the wheel.

Chapter Six

Zach carefully maneuvered the car into position as several dozen gawkers hovered nearby, waiting to get a closer look at what he was driving. Amy felt her pulse increase in speed—she wasn't sure if it was for the man or the car.

"For the car," she whispered, thinking no one would hear.

"For what car?" Mike asked from behind her.

"Oh, nothing." Amy turned around and looked at her boss.

Mike nodded toward the car Zach had just gotten out of. "Nice wheels, huh?"

"Very nice." Amy tried her best to keep her emotions from showing, but she wasn't sure she was doing such a good job.

"He won't have it here very long, but I think that's why he saved it for last. Cars like that are in demand with a certain breed of collectors."

Amy had seen all kinds of car collectors during the show this week. There were those who wanted only the very best, the cream of the crop. Some people were more budget conscious, and they leaned toward the more affordable models. And then there were several who were extremely discriminating, and they wanted only one model and often a specific year of that model. People in this last group came to the show, not expecting to find what they were looking for; they just didn't want to take a chance on missing anything.

Zach was instantly surrounded by men and women who had questions about his car. "That baby will be gone within the hour," Mike said.

"How can you tell?"

He pointed to several men who were on their cell phones. "See those guys over there?"

Amy nodded. "Yeah. What about them?"

"They're people who are hired by collectors to scout the shows and find what they're looking for. Obviously, their clients have plenty of money to spend, or they wouldn't be able to pay the hefty fee some of those guys get."

Just when she thought she knew what was going on, either Mike, Zach, or Patty told her something new. Antique car scouts? She had no idea this business was so big.

Exactly as Mike had predicted, Zach's car was gone

within the hour. Well, not gone, exactly, but there was a big "sold" sign in the window. That didn't keep the lookers away, though. They hovered around the car, and several of them asked to have their pictures taken behind the wheel.

"Why don't you go see what Zach wants?" Mike asked. "He's been trying to get your attention for a few minutes."

She begrudgingly obliged. All afternoon, Amy tried not to give Zach too much thought, but that was impossible with that flashy car and all the attention it drew.

"Did you want me?" Amy asked as she approached Zach at the opening of his booth.

"Yeah." Taking her by the hand, he pushed through the crowd and opened the car door. "Get in. I want a snapshot of you."

"Why me?" Amy said, doing as she was told.

"Because you're the classiest lady in the place, and I want a picture of my pride and joy, since I just sold her."

That was the nicest compliment Amy could ever remember getting. Zach had called her classy. She'd been born and raised in the wealthiest neighborhood of Nashville, but she'd never heard anyone call her classy, probably because everyone else came from the same roots as her.

Zach took several pictures of her, all of them in different positions. When he was finished, he nodded and smiled. "I think that's enough. I'll make sure you get one after they're developed."

"I'd appreciate that, Zach," she said softly, wishing her heart would stop pounding so hard.

"Better get back to work, or Mike will have me arrested for stealing your time."

Amy chuckled as she headed back to her station. Several customers and clients wanted pictures of the cars, and Mike was beginning to get a few of his own for his scrapbook. The cars in this show were almost like the dealers' babies, the way they showed pictures of them and gave detailed histories of where they'd been. She even thought the car scrapbooks were filled with more information than most baby books of first-born children.

"We're getting near the end of the show," Mike announced. "Just a couple more days, and it's over."

His voice sounded sad, but he was smiling. Amy never dreamed she'd dread something as much as she did her last day working for Mike.

"When's your next show?" she asked.

"Next month. I would ask for you, but it's in Florida, so I'll use an agency down there. Hotel costs are pretty steep around all the tourist attractions, so I can't afford to foot the bill. And I don't expect my models to spend all their money on living expenses."

Amy started to tell him she could afford her own hotel and that she was just doing this temp work to figure out what she wanted to do with her life, but she didn't. She didn't want him to know she was rich and had a trust fund worth more than most of the people in the room, combined.

Instead, she smiled and nodded. "Maybe I can work at the next one you have close by."

"Yes," he agreed. "I'd like that. I was hoping you wouldn't mind if I requested you by name."

"Hold on there, Mike," Zach said from behind. "I want Amy to work for me next time."

Mike spun around and snorted. "I thought you didn't think you needed a model to sell your cars, Zach."

"I didn't," Zach said. "But I do now. This business is getting mighty competitive, and I need the same edge all the rest of you have."

"If you want Amy, you'll have to beat me to the draw." Mike was teasing, but it still felt good to be in demand. "But that might be kinda hard since I'm calling Carol first thing Monday morning."

Zach grinned. "I already called her."

"Son of a gun," Mike grumbled with a good-natured edge. "I shoulda figured you'd go and do something like that."

Zach looked at Amy and saw the stunned look of bewilderment on her face. Hopefully, she wouldn't mind what he did. It was too late now, though. He'd called the temp agency that Mike had used to get Amy, and Carol was pleased that her new employee was working out so well.

"I thought you sold all your cars, Zach," Amy said.

Mike and Zach both burst into laughter. "No one in this business ever sells all his cars," Mike told her. "In fact, we have a list of people looking to sell us what they've got, and we turn more of them away than we can ever accept."

"Oh." Her eyes were focused on the floor. Zach couldn't tell whether she was upset or just thinking, processing all this new information. He knew she'd never been around antique cars before, but she sure had caught on mighty fast.

"Big difference between Mike and me is that I'll have you doing more talking to the customers." Zach figured it would be best if he kept the banter going to relax her a little.

"I let her talk to the customers," Mike argued.

"With price sheets?"

"Yep."

"Contracts?"

"Well, no, but I didn't hire her to sell."

Amy looked at Zach. "Even though she didn't have contracts, she's probably responsible for most of your sales this week."

"Yeah," Mike agreed. "You're probably right. I never would have gotten top dollar if it weren't for Amy. She lent a touch of class to the operation, and that speaks for itself."

"So, whaddya say, Amy?" Zach said. "Would you like to have an opportunity to earn a little commission on top of modeling?"

* * *

Again, Amy was tempted to tell him she wasn't doing this for the money, but before she let the cat out of the bag, she pulled her lips between her teeth and nodded. She had never sold anything but books before, but she was willing to learn. And she had to admit, being around these old cars had turned out to be quite a bit more fun than she'd imagined. It was almost like being in a car buff's amusement park. She saw the same gleam in customers' eyes as she'd seen in children's at Disney World.

During break, Patty was so excited she almost couldn't contain herself. "I found the perfect property, Amy. It's on the edge of Clearview, this side. They have twice as much property as I need, so all I have to do now is talk the owner into dividing it and selling me half."

"Why don't you buy the whole piece of property?" Amy asked.

Patty snorted. "I might have money, but I'm not filthy rich. They want an arm and a leg for that land."

Amy nodded and listened as Patty went on and on about how perfect the property was. Her excitement was contagious.

"Are there any existing buildings?" Amy asked.

"Just a double-wide mobile home that's used for offices. I figured I could leave that there and construct a garage in front of it. I'll need space for a desk and file cabinets, anyway."

Although Clearview seemed to have more than its share of mobile homes, she'd never been inside one.

They'd intrigued her, mainly because she couldn't imagine someone living in a house on wheels. Denise had explained that the word "mobile" was a misnomer because once the home was put on a lot, it was next to impossible to move again. And the wheels were generally taken off, and the structure was anchored to steel bolts in the ground.

"Sounds lovely, Patty. I'm so happy for you."

"There's only one problem." Patty's smile faded slightly as she thought for a moment. "I'm almost sure I'll need a business partner now. I already have more customers than I know what to do with. And I've promised them the moon. Once I get set up in business, I'm gonna hit the ground running."

"You say you need a partner to do the interiors of the cars?" Amy asked, making polite conversation.

"That and some of the office stuff. I'm terrible at keeping books."

After they went back to their booths, Amy immersed herself in her work. She was needed to pose for several of the newspapers that had sent reporters from across the state. She'd done this the second day of the show, but there were a few stragglers who arrived at the show in the last hours.

"Too bad they didn't get here in time for a picture of the car Zach just sold," Amy said.

Mike shook his head. "Yeah, that's too bad. But at least I still have this Mustang. It's a good idea to have a signature car that people associate with the dealer."

"How much would it take for you to part with the Mustang?" Amy asked.

When Mike quoted her a figure, she knew for certain that it was almost double the value in the antique car books. But she understood why he'd valued it so high. He didn't really want to part with it.

Amy had grown to appreciate the fine lines and well-maintained beauty and engine of the car. She'd watched enough ardent admirers lovingly stroke the sides and look at the engine. By Saturday morning, Amy wanted the Mustang. And from what she could see, she was the only person who was willing to pay the price.

Her big problem now was how to get possession of the car without Mike knowing she was the buyer. Not that she wanted to be deceitful about anything. She just didn't want to flaunt her money.

She asked for a late afternoon break on Saturday and called her brother. "Andrew, would it be too hard to get one of your friends to make an offer on a vintage Mustang for me?"

Andrew groaned. "What do you want with a car like that, Amy? You can barely maintain the one you have, and it's practically brand new."

"I just happen to know someone who's going to open a shop that specializes in antique cars."

"Oh, you do, do you?" he said.

"Let me speak to Denise, then," Amy said. "I know she'll at least listen to me."

"She's not here, but I'll see what I can do. It doesn't

make a lick of sense, but neither does the fact that you're so determined to work for a living."

"You're working, Andrew," she argued, "and you don't have to, either."

"That's different."

"Tell me how." Amy loved her brother, but she knew he was still being overprotective of her. One of these days she was going to make him stop.

"Uh, well . . ." His voice trailed off, and he cleared his throat. "Okay, Amy, I get your point. You need to do this for self-respect and to feel useful."

"Exactly." He was learning, she was proud to see.

"I'm sure I can find someone who'll bid on the car. What do we have to do?"

Amy explained how this could be done after the show. And she also told him that her name was *never* to be brought out during the negotiation.

"That's what doesn't make sense to me, but I guess you have your reasons," Andrew said.

"That's right. I have my reasons. And the first one is that I don't want anyone here to know about our family money."

"You sound ashamed of it," he said.

"Sometimes I am. All these people here are so nice, and they work so hard to make ends meet. And they have dreams that have to wait until they have enough money." Amy went on about how much she admired people who had to work for what they had.

"You're a good person, Amy," Andrew said. "And that's why I'm proud you're my sister."

"I'll remember you said that," she said with a chuckle. "Now I have to get back to my post."

For the remainder of her time there, Amy couldn't take her eyes off the Mustang. She hoped her brother would come through for her and find someone to do the deal.

"Nice, isn't she?" Mike asked.

He'd caught her staring at the car. "I've grown pretty attached to this car, Mike. I can see why you don't want to let her go. I'm kind of surprised no one has come close to your price."

"If someone's willing to pay what I'm asking, it won't be hard to let go," he said. "But I think it takes time for her to grow on someone. Take you, for instance."

"Me?"

"Yeah. When you first walked up, would you have even given her a second look?"

"Well, yes. Even my untrained eyes could see that there was something special about this car."

"Okay, okay, but would you have thought I was being reasonable with my asking price?" He stared at her, waiting for her answer.

"No, of course not. I thought you were nuts," Amy admitted.

"There ya go. Everyone else thinks I'm nuts, too, which is why I'll probably never sell her." He picked up a rag and began to wipe the side of the car, getting rid of imaginary fingerprints.

"Good rationale," she said. "But you may be surprised one of these days."

Mike stopped his circular motion with the rag. "Do you know something I don't know?"

She shrugged. "Not anything for sure."

He let out a sigh. "You had me scared there for a moment. But one thing's for certain."

"What's that?"

"If someone offers me my price, I'll jump on it, and I won't look back. Everything has its price."

Not everything, Amy thought. She'd heard that expression all her life, and many of her father's friends had taken advantage of that notion. Sure, it held true for some people, but she for one wasn't willing to give up certain ideals or valuables for any price. But then again, she'd never had to do without, so she couldn't very well put herself in anyone else's position, either.

"Zach's coming. Don't you two have a date tonight?"

Amy whipped around to see Zach coming up from behind with a grin on his face. "Since I don't have any inventory to bring back, we can take my truck. I'll have to drop off the trailer, but that won't take long."

"Are you sure you don't want me to drive?"

"Well, if you really want to," he said. "I don't mind."

"Must be nice to have a pretty lady offering to drive you around," Mike said.

Zach winked at Amy, increasing her pulse rate like only he knew how to do. "Yes, it would be nice."

"That settles it," Amy said. "I'll drive. Where do you want to go?"

He shrugged. "Plattsville doesn't exactly have the best nightlife in the world. They have a diner, a few fast food places out by the highway, and the Pine Room. Take your pick."

Amy really liked the ambiance of the Pine Room, but she wasn't sure if Zach could afford it. She would offer to pick up the tab, but she didn't want to offend him. After all, he was the one who'd asked her out.

"I really don't care," she said. "It's completely up to you."

Mike patted his chest. "Where were you when I was young, Amy? No woman ever offered to drive me anywhere I wanted to go."

Zach playfully punched Mike's shoulder. "That's because they had a hard time hitching up the horse and buggy." Turning to Amy, he added, "Most of these cars are probably younger than Mike."

Amy knew Zach was kidding. Mike belted out a deep belly laugh, and she smiled. The camaraderie shared by all these car buffs was really special, and she'd enjoyed being a part of it this past week.

"Since we enjoyed our meal so much at the Pine Room, why don't we go back?" Zach asked. "We can try something different."

"Sounds good to me," she said.

After she helped Mike clear off the table and pack

the paperwork in the back of his van, he told her he looked forward to seeing her again. "Too bad I didn't get to the agency before Zach, but maybe he'll let me borrow you if I need help closing on a big deal."

Amy smiled and gave him a hug. She really did like Mike. He was much more fun than she'd imagined he would be when she accepted the assignment.

"How about the car?" Amy asked, referring to the Mustang on the arena floor.

"I'll come back tomorrow afternoon and pick her up. Security will be here all night, so I don't have to worry," Mike said. This was the first time Amy had seen exhaustion in his eyes. It was like all the energy had drained from his body.

"Where's your car?"

"It's the red one over there," she said, pointing to a line of cars on the back row.

"The convertible?" he asked, his voice an octave higher. "I couldn't tell in the dark the other night."

"You sound surprised."

"I am," he admitted. "Somehow, I had you figured for a Volvo or BMW."

"Really?" she asked, giggling. He had no idea how close to the truth he'd been in that assumption. She'd grown up with Volvos, BMWs, and Mercedes, all driven by hired drivers.

With a devilish grin, he slipped his arm around her shoulders and gave her a squeeze. "No wonder I like you. You keep me guessing all the time." He glanced down and winked. "You're a lady of mystery."

If he only knew.

Chapter Seven

"I found someone to make an offer on that car you want," Andrew told Amy when she called him after she got home from her date. "But I want to know something first."

"Sure, what's that?"

"Why are you home so late? I thought you were finished early today."

"Andrew," she groaned. "Stop doing this. I'm a grown woman, and I don't need a curfew. Besides, I'm not exactly waltzing in during the wee hours of the night." She glanced at her watch. "It's only nine o'clock."

"The show was over at six, and it only takes half an hour at the most to get home." Andrew wasn't letting up; he was being relentless.

"I thought I told you I was going out to dinner with Zach."

"Zach?" Andrew asked. "You mean that auto mechanic."

"Don't be a snob, Andrew."

"I am not a snob. Some of my best friends are good with their hands. It's just that Dad—"

"Don't worry about Daddy. I'll take care of him if he asks."

"Okay, okay," Andrew finally said. "It doesn't sound serious, anyway, so I'll back off."

"Thank you," she said sarcastically. Then, she added, "Besides, he has his degree in industrial technology."

"Then why is he an auto mechanic?"

"Because he likes it."

Amy waited for a moment, thinking Andrew would make another comment, but he didn't. He was learning that she wouldn't tolerate him treating her like a child anymore.

"See you tomorrow in church?" Andrew finally asked.

"Of course. Why wouldn't you?"

"Hey, Amy, don't get so testy with me. I'm just looking after your best interest."

"You're just being my overprotective big brother is what you're doing."

"Guilty as charged."

After Amy got off the phone, she went straight to

bed. For the first time since her first full day on the arena floor, she got a good night's sleep.

"Hey, Amster," Denise said practically from across the Fellowship Hall in church. "How was the temp job?"

Amy grinned and gave the thumbs-up sign. She stood there and waited for Denise to high-tail it over to her.

"Tell me more about this hunk you met," Denise said in a conspiratorial tone.

"Who said anything about a hunk?"

"Come on, Amster. I'm not as big of a fool as you think I am. What's his name? Zach?"

Amy realized she'd been cornered, so she gave a brief description of Zachary Harper. She told Denise what he looked like as well as what he did for a living.

"Auto mechanic, huh?" Denise said as she looked up at the ceiling, deep in thought. "That might be a handy kind of guy to have around."

"Yes, I suppose so," Amy said in as noncommittal of a way as possible. "Did Andrew tell you what I asked him to do?"

Denise's eyes lit up mischievously. "Yeah, and I think it's so cool. Know who he got to do it?"

"No telling," Amy replied.

"David."

"David? You mean David Hadaway?"

"The one and only."

"Oh, man," Amy groaned. "I can't believe he got a preacher involved in my scheme."

"Scheme?" Bethany Hadaway's voice came up from the side. "Did someone mention a scheme?" Her eyes were lit up as brightly as Denise's.

Amy had heard about Denise's and Bethany's escapades as teenagers, but she'd also heard they'd grown up and repented. Obviously, the danger of a scheme still sounded alluring to both of them.

Denise turned to Bethany and told her about the car Amy wanted to buy. Bethany looked puzzled.

"Why don't you just make the offer yourself?" Bethany asked.

Amy didn't even have a chance to open her mouth before Denise answered for her. "She doesn't want these car dealers to know she has money."

"You shouldn't try to hide anything like that, Amy," Bethany advised. "I'm not saying you should flaunt it, but don't turn it into a big secret. People don't want to think they've been deceived."

With a shrug, Amy said, "I don't think it really matters. But just in case, I'd much rather not tell the owner of the car I'm the one who's willing to pay him his exorbitant price."

"Exorbitant?" Bethany shrieked. "You mean you're paying his asking price? You're not haggling?"

"No, he's firm on that price because he really doesn't want to get rid of the car."

Bethany shook her head. "This makes absolutely no sense."

"You're right," Denise agreed. "No sense at all."

"But I want the car." Amy felt like a stubborn little rich girl who had to have her way, but it really wasn't like that at all. She'd been bitten by the vintage car bug, and she really did love that red Mustang convertible. It meant a lot for her to get it.

"What kind of car is it?" Bethany asked.

"It's a red convertible," Denise replied.

Bethany's forehead creased in confusion. "I thought you already had a red convertible. Why would you want another one?"

"It's a Mustang," Denise said in a sing-song tone.

Obviously, Andrew had told Denise all about the car since she knew so much about it. She wondered what else they had said about this deal.

"Ooh," Bethany said with a look of understanding. "I've heard that the old Mustangs are worth quite a bit. Matter of fact, I just happen to know someone who collects old cars, and she's had a few Mustangs through the years."

Denise turned and looked at Bethany. "Who's that?"

"Remember Patty O'Neill?"

"Oh, yeah, that's right," Denise replied. "She was always hanging out with the boys. Best tree climber in town from what I remember."

"You know Patty?" Amy exclaimed. "I worked with her at the car show."

"How's she doin'?" Denise asked.

Amy told them all about the car Patty sold and how she was now going to be able to start the car restoration business she'd always wanted. "When I first met Patty, I thought she was just a model, but she only does that to help pay for her car hobby."

"That's way cool," Bethany said. "Last time I saw her she looked really good, nothing like the pigtailed little monster from when we were kids."

"Monster?" Amy asked. The Patty she'd met was nothing like a monster. She was one of the sweetest people she'd ever met.

Both Denise and Bethany burst into laughter. "She could beat up any boy in school. No one dared to cross her."

Shaking her head, Amy chuckled. "That's hard to imagine after the week I spent with her. She's obviously changed."

"Yeah, a lot of people change, don't they?" Denise looked back and forth between Bethany and Amy.

Amy had heard all about the tragedy and trauma Bethany had gone through with her mother dying and her grandmother having a stroke a year later. She'd been upset and bitter, but Denise and David had been extremely kind, and they'd helped her through the difficult times.

And her own change had taken place over the period of time she'd worked in Denise's bookstore. She'd learned to stand on her own two feet, she'd learned to drive, and she'd undergone a physical transformation that almost put her brother in apoplectic shock. But once he got used to the new look, he actually seemed to approve. Then, he married Denise, making Amy's life more fun. She'd always wanted a sister, and now she had one.

Denise chuckled. "Amy, I wonder what your dad would do with a daughter like Patty. Her own father wasn't sure what to do with her after her mother died."

"Yeah, that's probably why she was such a tomboy. She was raised by her father and two brothers. They taught her everything they knew, which was sports and cars." Bethany was always the one to look at reasons why people did the things they did.

"Hey, ladies," Andrew said as he joined them, draping one arm around his wife and the other around his sister. He looked at Amy. "Did Denise tell you that David is going to be your car buyer?"

Amy nodded. "I hope he understands he's not supposed to tell the dealer who's really behind the deal."

"Don't worry about that. As far as David's concerned, I'm the one buying the car," Andrew said.

Bethany backed away from the group, laughing. "This is getting way too complicated for me. I'm outta here."

Later on in the afternoon, everyone convened at the Hadaways' house, like they did most Sundays. Amy brought bread from the bakery, Bethany's grandmother Gertie brought dessert, and Denise and Andrew brought a vegetable casserole. David cooked the meat as usual, and Denise was adding a few steamed vegetables to the mix as they filled the table with more food than any group this size could possibly eat.

After the blessing, Gertie told story after story about Bethany and Denise as little girls, most likely embellishing them as she went. Everyone was used to it, and they laughed all the way through the meal. This was one of the most special times for Amy—coming over here and enjoying the company of her friends. The only thing that would make it even more fun was if she had Zach by her side.

Just the thought of Zach jolted her from her present reality. "What's wrong, Amy?" Denise asked with concern. "You look like you just saw a ghost."

"N-no, I just thought of something, that's all."

Denise smiled and winked. Amy could tell she knew. That only made it more difficult to get through dinner.

"You mean you actually got an offer on the Mustang?" Zach asked Mike. "For the full asking price?"

With a crisp nod, Mike replied, "Yep. Even I can't believe it. I have no idea who'd want that car so bad."

"Ya gonna take it?"

"Of course. I'd be a fool not to."

Zach inhaled and let it out through his nose. "I'd like to have that car myself, but I'm not about to pay what you're asking."

"She's a good car," Mike said. "But if you'd offered less than my asking price, I might have considered it. I know you'd take good care of her."

"I couldn't do that to a good friend," Zach said.

"When ya gonna see Amy again?" Mike had blind-sided Zach by changing the subject so quickly.

"I don't know. Maybe not until the next show."

"Don't be stubborn, Zach. Girls like Amy don't come into a guy's life everyday, ya know."

"Yeah, I know. But I've been burned once already. Not gonna let it happen again."

Mike took a step back and glared at Zach. "She's not like Melody."

"You're right. She's nothing like Melody, or I never would have asked her out."

"And she's not likely to play you like Melody did."

Zach had heard enough of a lecture from his dear friend. "Enough about Amy. I'll let you know if something happens, but I highly doubt anything will."

With a sly grin, Mike shook his head. "Don't bet the farm on that statement, Zach. Love has a funny way of creeping up on you. Trust me. I know. When my sweet Helen walked into my life, nothing was ever the same."

Zach reached out and patted Mike's back. "Helen was truly one of a kind. Fine woman."

There was nothing else Zach could say about Mike's wife of forty years. She had died two years ago of cancer, and Mike had vowed to worship her memory for the rest of his life. Zach couldn't blame him, either. They had that special unique relationship that was rare.

"So, when ya gonna give up the car?" Zach asked.

Mike shrugged. "Some preacher from Clearview is

stopping by my office with a cashier's check for the full amount next week."

"Someone from Clearview is buying the car?"

"Yeah. Reverend David Hadaway. Know him?"

Zach thought for a moment before he folded his arms across his chest and shook his head. "No, I don't recall anyone by that name."

"He must have money or the ability to get his hands on a lot of it," Mike said with a snort. "Unlike any preacher I've ever known."

"Maybe he's been saving for the perfect car."

"That must be it," Mike agreed.

Amy headed straight for the mansion where her brother and Denise now lived. It was hard for her to believe she'd moved into this stodgy neighborhood that was almost a carbon copy of where she'd lived in Nashville. The big difference was, her home in Nashville had been filled with love. This house was just big and hollow-feeling. Even Denise didn't like it, and that was why it was on the market. The realtor had told them it might take a while to sell, since "prospects for houses like this don't grow on trees."

Hopefully, it would sell soon so she could give Denise her cottage back. Even Andrew loved the house that Denise had transformed into a cheerful little home with bright colors and flowers in every color imaginable, planted in beds throughout the yard.

Then, Amy would buy her own house and consult Denise about ways to turn it into a home. She'd discovered that she actually liked small houses more than large ones because they felt cozy.

She wondered where Zach lived. He'd mentioned an apartment, but she didn't know where exactly. Clearview and Plattsville had grown with new industry coming to the area, so developers had lined the outskirts of both areas with multi-unit dwellings with amenities that sounded like fun. Perhaps she'd live in an apartment for a while to be around more people her own age.

First thing Monday morning, she reported to Carol at the temp agency. "Hi, Amy," Carol said, smiling. "You made quite a hit at the antique car show."

"It was fun."

"Yeah, I bet it was. So many good-looking young men milling around." Amy noticed a twinkle in Carol's eye.

"I worked hard, but I liked it," Amy said, trying to change the subject. She didn't want to have to answer any personal questions.

Carol pulled a slip of paper from beneath a stack. "I have a job for you, if you're not too tired from last week. Since you're getting paid time and a half overtime from the car show, I wasn't sure if you wanted to take this."

Amy reached out and took the job slip Carol had offered. "Yes, I want to take it." She looked down and saw the word "receptionist." Her heart fell in a disappointed thud.

"All you have to do is answer phones, greet people

when they come in, and pull files for appointments. It's a dentist's office, and their regular receptionist is taking a week off to help her sister with her baby."

Amy couldn't think of anything less exciting than working in a dentist's office. Not only that, it didn't tie in with her plan of finding a business she might want to get into. But Carol needed her people to go on the jobs she assigned, so she nodded.

"I'll go."

"Good," Carol said with a relieved smile. "The work's not hard, and the rest of the people in the office are pretty friendly. You might want to bring a book or something to do because there are times it might get pretty boring."

Oh, great. A boring job. That's all Amy needed after the exciting week she had.

When Amy arrived at the dentist's office, an older woman greeted her at the counter. She handed the woman the slip and said, "I'm here to report to work as receptionist."

"Come on back," the woman told her. "I'm Barbara, and I'm the office manager."

Once Amy was behind the counter, Barbara offered her a chair at the glass window and gave her a brief lesson on how they liked their phones answered. Then, she took Amy on a tour of the office and said, "When we're ready to take each patient, all you have to do is say his or her name, lead them to the numbered office we tell you, and wait for the next patient. Most of the time I answer the phone, but if I'm busy, you'll handle that. Here's the appointment book." She showed her the way they scheduled people, which took all of five minutes. There was nothing difficult about this job—or fun, either. No one liked going to the dentist.

Fortunately, Amy's hours weren't bad. She arrived at nine o'clock, had an hour for lunch and a fifteen-minute break each afternoon. She went home at four-thirty. The week flew by.

"How'd it go?" Denise asked when she called late Friday afternoon.

"It was okay, but I know for sure I don't want to be a dentist now."

Denise laughed. "Can't say I blame you. Did Carol tell you where you are working next week?"

"I told her I'd like a couple days off, so she said she'd look for something that wasn't a week-long assignment."

"That's the good thing about Carol," Denise said. "She seems to have just what you need, when you need it."

"I don't see how she does it. I never realized there were so many different businesses in such a small town."

"Clearview won't remain a small town at the rate it's growing," Denise said sadly.

"I understand why everyone wants to move here. I love living here."

Denise changed the subject. "Have you heard from Zach?"

"Not since last week." Amy couldn't help that her voice sounded clipped.

"Don't want to talk about it?"

"Not really."

"Okay," Denise said softly. "How's the new car?"

"It's beautiful," Amy said. She'd put the car in the detached garage behind the house to protect it from the elements. It was so beautiful she was almost afraid to drive it.

"Wanna take me for a ride in it sometime?"

"Sure." Amy hadn't even ridden in it other than to garage it, but she knew that was silly. Even though it was a collector's item, it was still only a car.

The weekend seemed longer than usual, since Denise and Andrew had decided to do a little mission work with Bethany and David. She could have called Connie or Phyllis, but she figured she might as well rest and regroup. Working at different jobs, no matter how easy they were, was pretty tiring.

She did laundry and cleaned the house on Saturday, and on Sunday she went to church to hear the pastor David had called to fill in while he was gone. Bethany's grandmother Gertie waved and gestured for her to join her in the pew. It was a relief to have someone to sit with.

"How's the workin' girl?" Gertie asked, grinning.

Amy shrugged. "I'm okay. I still haven't found what I want to do with my life."

Gertie patted her on the leg. "Don't worry. Things

like this take time. You're young, and you have your whole life ahead of you. Don't rush yourself."

It was nice to be with someone Gertie's age who understood what she was going through. Gertie seemed to have a very strong knowledge of what was really important in life. She'd come near death a couple years ago, according to Denise, and she valued every moment she had on earth. Amy aspired to be more like her.

Carol had found a two-day job for Amy, starting on Tuesday. "It's not exactly the plushest office, but it's all I could do with short notice."

"Where is it?" Amy asked. The job slip only said "Tom's."

"Tom's Garage is on Fourth Street, about a block from the downtown area. His wife normally sits at the desk, but her mother's in town this week, and they want to go shopping. She's a good friend of mine, and when I told her about you, she said you could have her job for a couple days."

Amy smiled at Carol. "Thanks. I have no idea how you do it, but you're good."

"I've been in this business practically all my life, and I know everyone in town. You'll like Tom. He likes to kid around and tell jokes. Some of them are pretty silly, but they'll make you laugh."

That sounded much better than being a receptionist in a dentist's office, where people walked in the door, shaking with fear. "I like silly jokes," Amy said.

Now, she had the rest of Monday to find something

to do. She headed over to Denise's bookstore to see how the weekend mission trip went.

"Oh, Amy, you should have seen them," Denise said, tears forming in her eyes. "Some of those children were so confused."

They'd spent Saturday and Sunday talking to runaways in Atlanta, and they'd offered suggestions on how to find shelter until they could get their personal problems straightened out. David really had a heart for children, and he did things like this every chance he got. Amy admired him and Bethany for what they were doing.

"Maybe some day I can go with you," Amy said. In the past, she'd never imagined herself wanting to stay in a run-down hotel, just so she could talk to some smart-mouthed kids. But she'd changed, and she knew that she really could make a difference in people's lives.

"Oh, Amy," Denise said, "I almost forgot to tell you. Some guy stopped by and asked about you."

"Some guy?" Who could that have been?

"Yeah. He didn't give me his name, but I suspect it might have been someone from the car show."

"Zach?" Amy asked before she had a chance to catch herself.

Denise grinned. "I'm not sure, but he was mighty handsome."

Chapter Eight

"He didn't leave his name?" Amy couldn't control herself now. She had to know.

"No. When I asked him, he just shook his head and said he'd look up your phone number and call."

Amy groaned. "My number's unlisted, remember? Daddy doesn't think it's a good idea for a woman living alone to have her number in the phone book."

"Trust me," Denise said with a sly smile. "He can find you if he really wants to." She had a twinkle in her eye that seemed suspicious.

"Did you give him my number?" Amy asked, now hopeful that she'd hear from Zach soon.

"Me?" Denise said in mock surprise and hurt. "I'd never do anything like that. Your father would kill me."

Amy's heart fell again. "If it was Zach, it would have been okay."

"I sent him to your brother," Denise said. "I figured it would be okay if he gave him your number."

"Oh, no. That's the worst thing you could have done. Andrew doesn't think I'm grown up, and he'll tell him to get lost."

"I don't think so," Denise said, one eyebrow arched. "I called Andrew and told him he'd better behave. Or else."

Amy knew that Denise had a way of getting Andrew to do what she wanted. There was that tone of voice, that look, that manner of knowing what she was doing, that let people know she meant business. Andrew trusted and relied on Denise, which really surprised Amy in the beginning because he'd always been so protective towards women. He was still protective towards Denise, but he treated her with utmost respect. Denise never would have married him if he hadn't.

Well, now all Amy could do was sit back and wait. She glanced at her watch and figured it was time to get home so she could get a couple days' worth of clothes ready for work. On her way to her car, she stopped by the bakery and picked up a half dozen of her favorite muffins.

The instant she turned down her street, Amy spotted Zach's truck in her driveway. He was just sitting there, waiting. Tempting as it was to step harder on the accelerator, she didn't. She moved at her regular speed and pulled in right behind him.

He hopped out of the truck as soon as she turned off her engine. "Amy, I've had a heck of a time finding you." His face looked even better than she remembered.

"Did my brother tell you where I live?" Amy was surprised if he had, but she had no idea of any other way he could have gotten her address.

With a chuckle, he nodded. "That brother of yours is a nice guy, but he's about the most protective man I've ever seen." Zach's gaze dropped to the ground, then met hers again. "But I can understand how he feels. I'd feel the same way if I had a sister like you."

Amy wasn't sure right away whether to take that as a compliment, but she figured she might as well. No sense inviting worry. "How did you know to stop by the bookstore?"

"That part was easy. I just headed straight for the downtown area and asked some of the business owners I used to know. They pointed me in her direction."

"Do you know a lot of people in Clearview?" Neither Denise nor Bethany knew Zach.

"Several, yes."

"Denise has lived in Clearview all her life, and she didn't remember you from school."

"I went to school in the county because we lived on a farm. Clearview had their own schools."

"Oh." Amy stood there, her purse hanging from her shoulder, Zach standing there staring at her.

"Would you mind if I come in?" he finally asked.

"Oh, no, not at all," she replied. What had she been thinking? "Want some tea?"

"Sure."

They sat in the bright yellow kitchen and sipped tea while they chatted about the car show from a week and a half ago. It had been considered a whopping success.

Amy didn't mention the car she'd bought, and she was glad she'd put it in the garage. He was close friends with Mike, and for now, she didn't want to let anyone outside the family know she was the proud new owner of the vintage car.

After an hour of small talk, Zach stood up. "Listen, Amy, the reason I stopped by was to see if you were doing anything Friday night."

She licked her lips that had suddenly gone dry. "Uh, no, I don't have anything going on that I know of."

"Would you like to do something with me?"

Amy nodded. She couldn't talk.

His face lit up in a smile. "Good. I'll be here around six o'clock, and we can find something to do in Clearview, if that's okay with you."

"Yes, that would be just fine," she said, falling back on one of her old society responses.

He looked at her, puzzled, then he backed toward the door. "Guess I'd better be going. I'm sure you have things to do."

After Zach left, Amy realized that the whole time he was in the house, she'd been in a state of shock. Her reactions were almost mechanical. Hopefully, he wouldn't read into them, but he was astute. He'd probably wonder what was wrong.

If Zach didn't know better, he'd think Amy was trying to hide something from him. But what kinds of secrets could she have that would make her act this way?

She seemed happy to see him, but she was obviously nervous about having him there. He hadn't intended to ask her out so soon, but the instant the thought had popped into his head, he was helpless to stop it from reaching his mouth. And he was overjoyed at the prospect of being with her on Friday night.

The problem was, where would they go? Clearview had a couple of small restaurants and a bunch of fast food places. Oh, and there was the Burger Barn. He had made a few memories there. Back when he was a teenager, he and some friends would drive through the parking lot, "cruising for chicks," as they called it. But they never did anything but look. The girls they saw from Clearview High intimidated them. And the girls from the school where he attended all lived on neighboring farms, and he looked at them more as sisters than potential girlfriends.

He'd have to ask Amy what she wanted to do. Maybe they could grab a quick bite to eat, then go to the movie downtown. He could suggest taking her to the drive-in theater that played second-run movies, but he didn't want to risk offending her.

No matter how many times he tried to shove Amy

Mitchell from his mind, Zach came up short. She popped into his thoughts at the strangest of times, like when he drove by Mike's business, or when he heard someone mention the Pine Room. And if someone brought up anything relating to the car show, watch out! Amy's image flashed into his brain, and he couldn't let go of it for hours!

He remembered the first time he'd seen her sitting on the back of his car. She was so cute. Her indignation only enhanced his attraction to her when she stormed off to where she was supposed to report.

Now, when he pictured her in his mind, she was either sitting on his car, or she was behind the wheel of Mike's red Mustang. It was sad that Mike had sold that car; it looked so right with Amy. In fact, in his mind, the perfect ad for vintage cars would have involved a picture of Amy in that Mustang.

At least he had a date to see her again. He drove directly to Mike's house to let him know.

"Zach!" Mike answered the door wearing cutoffs and a ratty T-shirt. "Come on out back. I wanna show you something."

Mike led Zach around to the back of the house, where he had constructed a three-car carport adjacent to his detached two-car garage. Generally, all stalls were filled, but today, there were only two cars. Mike's inventory was low.

"Look at this, will ya?" Mike said, pointing to a bright blue '57 Chevrolet.

"She's a beaut," Zach agreed. "Needs a little work, though."

"Yeah, I figured I better find something to keep me busy and keep my mind off the Mustang. I'm really gonna miss that car."

"Me, too," Zach said. He shoved his hands in his pockets and thought about why he'd come. He hadn't consciously thought about why he wanted to see Mike, but now he knew why he was there. "I saw Amy."

Mike jerked his head up and looked directly at Zach. "You did? How is she?"

With a noncommittal shrug, Zach replied, "She seems okay."

"You like her, don't you?"

"Yeah, I guess."

"No, Zach." Mike took a step toward him. "I mean, you *really* like her."

"Haven't decided yet."

"She's not Melody. Don't hold what that woman did to you against all females." Mike had offered many words of advice to Zach, but most of the time it was about cars, not women.

"It's hard, man," Zach said as he pulled one hand out of his pocket and rested it against the carport pole. "That woman really shook me up."

"I know she did, but it's better that she did it before the wedding than what some women do and tell you she never really loved you after you've been married a few years."

"Yeah, I s'pose you're right."

"I know I'm right, Zach. She did you a favor."

Zach snorted. "Sure didn't feel like it at the time."

"So, where ya takin' her?"

Again, Zach shrugged. "I dunno. Maybe out for a bite to eat and to a movie."

"I never did like going to a movie back when I was courting my wife. Too hard to talk."

"Hadn't thought about that."

Mike snickered. "But on the other hand, if you see a horror movie, she'll grab your hand and want to snuggle."

They moved away from the carport and toward the front yard in silence. When they got to the front yard, Mike gestured toward the house. "Wanna go inside for something to drink?"

"No, I guess I better be going." Zach took a couple steps toward his truck, then turned and faced Mike who was standing there watching him. "Know any good horror flicks playing on Friday?"

Mike howled with laughter and waved. Zach got in his truck and headed for home.

He'd have to think about what Mike said. Should he try to forget about what Melody had done to him and see where he wound up with Amy? Or should he continue guarding his heart and let Amy prove that she wouldn't hurt him? Somehow, that didn't sound right. But then again, the idea of going through the pain of rejection was as bad as it got.

* * *

Amy actually had fun working for Tom. He seemed to know everyone in town, including Patty. She wondered if he knew Zach, but she didn't ask. That might open some questions that she wasn't ready for.

Most of the people who came to the shop either had cars with problems, or they wanted him to just take a look at something that was making a sound. She even delighted in the sound effects they made as they tried to help Tom identify what the problem was.

"Was that a 'ping' or a 'fwang'?" he asked one woman.

The woman whose four-year-old car was making an odd sound thought for a moment before she nodded. "I think it was more of a 'fwang.' "

"Then I have a feeling I know what the problem is," Tom said.

Amy had to bite her lip to keep from laughing. But the joke was on her when Tom came out from beneath the hood and nodded. "Just what I thought. You were smart to bring it in. It's a small problem now, but it would get worse if you ignored it."

So far, all the car people Amy had met were incredibly honest and nice. Her respect for this business had grown tremendously since the beginning of the car show.

"I'm not the best mechanic in town," Tom admitted to her on Wednesday, right before she was about to leave, "but I know what my limitations are. And I only fix what I understand. If there's something too difficult to diagnose, I send 'em over to Patty. Now there's an ace mechanic."

Amy was amazed that such a beautiful, graceful woman knew her way around cars so well. But why not? All it took was a good mind for logic and an interest in what makes car engines work to be a mechanic.

"I heard she's thinkin' about going into business for herself," Tom said as he handed her the signed job slip that she needed to give to Carol before she got paid. "Know anything about that?"

With a quick nod, Amy said, "Just that she's looking for land to put her garage on."

"I sure do hope she finds something good. Location is everything. Tell her I said so."

Tom smiled, shook Amy's hand, and went back inside. Amy left and headed straight for the temp agency, where she turned in her slip to Carol.

"How was it?" Carol asked.

"I had a wonderful time. Tom made the job easy, and there was never a dull moment."

Carol studied Amy for a moment, then looked down at her calendar. "I'm not sure where I'm going to send you next week, but I'll find something good. Denise told me that you're thinking about opening your own business, and you're looking for something that interests you. I'll have to keep that in mind."

Amy smiled back at her and nodded. "Thanks, Carol. Give me a call and let me know when you have something."

All the way home, Amy couldn't get over how much fun she'd had working for Tom at his garage and for Mike at the car show. If she didn't know better, she'd be seriously thinking about doing something with cars. Wouldn't her daddy just die if she did that? His daughter, the auto mechanic! How would he explain that to his buddies at the country club?

The light on the answering machine was blinking when she walked in the door. She punched the "play" button and turned up the volume so she could hear her messages as she got something to drink.

There were three calls. The first message was from her father, telling her he wanted to visit for a day next weekend. Then, Andrew had called and told her he'd spoken to their dad. The last message was from Denise, who said they needed to talk and to not speak with anyone until she called her first.

"What's up, Denise?" Amy asked the instant her sister-in-law answered the phone.

"Your father's coming to stay with us next weekend."

"Like not this weekend, but next?"

"That's right," Denise said. "In a week and a half."

Amy let out a sigh of relief. Good thing he wasn't coming this weekend. She had a date with Zach.

"Is there a problem?" Amy asked.

"I'm not sure, but I have a feeling your father's gonna try to talk you into moving back to Nashville."

"Why?"

"He's worried about you."

"Why?" Amy hated that she sounded like a warped CD, but she couldn't imagine why her father would be worried enough to try to talk her into moving back to Nashville. He knew she was happy here.

"Probably because he wants to make Andrew an offer with his company, and he knows Andrew won't go unless you do."

Amy gulped. So it was about more than just her. Why did she have to have this kind of pressure, just when she was finding her stride?

"Do you want to move?" Amy asked.

"Not really," Denise said. "I've lived in Clearview all my life, but if that's what Andrew really wants, I'll do it. Then there's the bookstore to think about."

"Everyone in town depends on you, Denise. You have the only bookstore in Clearview."

"I know, but I'm sure I could sell it pretty fast if we decided to move. Either that, or I could hire someone to manage it."

Amy groaned. Sounded to her like this topic had been discussed for a while, and she was the only one in the dark.

"You don't want to move, either, so what's the problem?" Denise asked.

"Obviously, you don't know how persuasive my father can be."

"Oh, I think I know," Denise said in her matter-of-fact tone. "I had a dad just like him, remember? His word was always final. Even though I never doubted his love, he tried everything he could think of to get me to do his bidding."

All Amy saw when she looked at Denise was a very strong woman who had more sense than anyone else she knew. It was hard to imagine anyone else running her life.

"But I didn't let him get the best of me," Denise said with a chuckle. "I always hugged him and told him I loved him, then I went about my business and did whatever I wanted to do."

Now *that* sounded just like the Denise Amy knew. And she wanted to be more like her.

"Your father loves you, Amy," Denise continued. "I'm sure there's a way you can convince him you want to stay here and that it's the best thing for both of you."

Amy laughed, a caustic edge in the tone that she hadn't intended to get out. "What's best for Daddy and what's best for me might be two completely different things."

"Maybe not, Amy," Denise said slowly. "Once he gets used to your independence, he'll probably really like the new relationship."

"We'll see," Amy said. She wasn't in the mood to argue. "So, what's on the agenda while they're here?"

"I thought we might have a little dinner party with a few close friends," Denise said. "He told Andrew to make sure David, Bethany, and Gertie were invited."

Amy remembered how well her dad got along with the preacher and his family. That gave him a little comfort, knowing that Amy hadn't fallen in with the "wrong" crowd.

"You might want to bring a date, too," Denise added. "How about asking Zach?"

"You're kidding, right?" Amy said.

"No. I think that would be nice."

"Do you realize what my father would do if he knew I was dating an auto mechanic?"

"C'mon, Amy, give your father credit for being a decent person. He doesn't care what someone does for a living."

"He doesn't as long as I'm not dating him," Amy said. "But he wants to hand-pick whomever I get serious about."

"Oh," Denise said, her voice raised an octave. "I didn't realize you and Zach were serious already."

Amy felt herself stiffen. She hadn't been aware of how she'd sounded. Was there something her subconscious was trying to tell her?

Chapter Nine

Amy quickly caught herself and tried to back-pedal. "That's not what I mean."

"Exactly what did you mean?" Denise asked slowly.

"It's just that . . ." She wasn't sure what she meant. "It's just that whenever I went out with someone back in Nashville, my dad gave me the third degree about the guy and his family. He wanted to know all the details, like where he lived, who his parents were, what he did for a living. All the usual stuff."

"Have you thought that he just wanted to know about the guy and wanted to make sure you weren't with some psychopath?"

There she goes, Amy thought, getting all wise again. Maybe Denise was right.

"I don't know. Let me think about it," Amy said.

"But count me in to bring something. Do you need dessert or bread?"

"Andrew and I were thinking a backyard barbecue would be fun. That way, we can all wear jeans and eat on the picnic table that almost never gets used."

"Sounds good to me," Amy said. "Just make sure to tell Daddy to bring something besides his suits."

Denise laughed. Amy wondered if Denise knew just how stodgy her dad really was. No matter how much she loved him, she couldn't ever remember seeing him relax and just enjoy life.

"I'll have Andrew talk to him. In the meantime, think about what I said. Zach wouldn't do anything to embarrass you. David said he's a pretty cool guy."

"Yes, he is pretty cool," Amy admitted. She left out the fact that he might be a little too cool for her dad. Besides, she still didn't want Zach to know she came from a wealthy family, but she didn't tell Denise, who thought that was ridiculous.

"So, what are you planning to do with him on Friday night?" Denise asked.

"How do you know about Friday?" Amy couldn't believe how fast word traveled in Clearview.

"Carol said that the guy you worked for at the car show told her."

"Mike?"

"Yeah," Denise said. "I think that's his name."

So Zach had talked to Mike about it. She wondered who else he'd told.

"I'm not sure where we're going, but I'll tell you all about it Saturday."

"You better," Denise said. "I want every single last detail, all the way down to what you order for dinner."

Amy felt herself relax. This was Denise at her finest. "Okay, okay, I'll take notes."

"Good girl."

After they hung up, Amy let out a deep sigh. She had no idea what to do about her parents' visit. Should she invite Zach to dinner? Or should she go alone? The advantage of going alone was that she wouldn't risk her father interrogating Zach about his intentions. But if she brought Zach, he wouldn't have as much of a chance to corner her about moving back to Nashville.

At least she had some time to think about what to do. Maybe the date wouldn't go very well, and there would be no reason to ask Zach. She'd have to wait, at least until Friday night.

All doubt about whether things would go well flew out the window the instant she saw him. Zach came up the sidewalk wearing khaki slacks, a navy polo shirt, and conservative shoes. Her father would definitely approve. And to top it off, he looked even better than he had the first time she'd seen him.

"Where would you like to go, Amy?" he asked as soon as she opened the door. "I drove one of my classic cars so you wouldn't have to ride in the truck."

"But I like your truck," Amy replied, leaning to the side to get a better look at what he was driving. The really cool thing about going out with a vintage car dealer was that he always seemed to have a new set of wheels.

"Next time." He offered his arm, and together, they walked out to the passenger side of the shiny white Cadillac convertible. "You'll have to settle for good old-fashioned luxury tonight."

Amy slid into the passenger seat and took a good long look around the interior of the car. There was enough daylight left to see that the vehicle was immaculate. The upholstery was well-maintained leather without a single crack. She really loved the way it felt riding in something that was made back in her parents' day.

"This is absolutely incredible," she told Zach when he got in.

With a grin, he said, "I thought you might like it. Now, where to?"

"Hmm." Amy made an exaggerated gesture, putting her finger to her chin and widening her eyes. "How about the Burger Barn?"

"The Burger Barn?" he asked incredulously. "Why the Burger Barn?"

"Denise told me that's where people in Clearview go to be seen."

"Teenagers, maybe."

"I feel like a teenager tonight," Amy said with enthusiasm. "Let's go to there and drive through the parking lot a few times before we go in."

"Okay," he said, shaking his head and chuckling. "The Burger Barn, it is."

Just as she'd imagined, all heads turned when they drove into the parking lot of the old fast food restaurant. Amy even recognized a few of the people, including some teenagers from church.

"Cool car," one guy from her Sunday school class said as they walked past him.

Amy just grinned and waved. She loved all the attention for something besides herself. The feeling of having people look at the car she was riding in rather than pointing their finger and saying, "There goes the Mitchell girl. You know, the one who lives in Belle Monde," was such a rush. It was great!

"What'll you have?" Zach asked with one brow raised.

"Same thing you have," she replied.

"Okay, four chili cheesedogs coming right up. Onion rings or fries?"

"Onion rings." Amy thought for a moment before she said, "I only want one chili cheesedog."

Zach laughed. "Okay, three chili cheesedogs, two onion rings, and what to drink?"

"Orange slushy."

"Sounds good," he said as he headed toward the counter. "I'll have that, too. Why don't you find us a booth while I place the order?"

Amy quickly found a seat where she could look out the window. There was a crowd around Zach's car, people of all ages admiring the lines and finish.

"Do all your cars get this kind of attention?" she asked.

"Most of them do. What happens with cars when they age is that they either fall apart, or they become collectors' items. Only the very best wind up in the car shows I do."

"How about Patty and Mike?"

"They're very ethical car people."

"I think it's great that Patty is a mechanic," Amy said. "I wonder how she'll do with her restoration business."

Zach shrugged. "I spoke with her yesterday, and she said she's going to have to find a business partner to make it work."

"Did she go ahead and buy that land she was talking about?"

"Not yet. The owner won't sell half. It's all or nothing."

"So let me see if I've got this straight. Not only does she have to find an investor for her business, she has to find someone who's looking for commercial real estate?"

"You got it." Zach popped an onion ring into his mouth, chewed, and swallowed. "How's your dinner?"

"Good." Amy's mind was whirring with different ideas about what she could do to help Patty. But how could she do anything without letting on that she had money?

Leaning forward, Zach looked deep into her eyes. "Whatcha thinking?"

She shook her head. "I was just thinking it would be nice for Patty to find a business partner who could afford to buy the whole piece of real estate." That wasn't a lie; it was part of what she'd been thinking. She'd left out the part about her considering being the silent investor.

"Do you know anyone who'd be willing to take a chance on Patty's business venture?" Zach was still watching her, studying her with intense interest.

"I might." Before he could ask another question, she took another huge bite of her chili cheesedog.

After they finished dinner, they had to wade through the people to get to their car. A new crowd had formed around the Cadillac, and several of the guys had questions. Zach was patient and seemed to enjoy answering them.

After a half dozen different questions, he glanced over at her and said, "Are you okay, Amy?"

She nodded. Not only was she okay, she loved every minute of it. The more she was around old cars, the more she liked them.

Finally, they managed to get away. "Where would you like to go now?"

Amy shrugged. "I'm not sure what there is to do on a Friday night in Clearview. I haven't exactly gotten into the nightlife here."

Zach let his head fall back, and he laughed. "Nightlife? The only thing I can think of is going to a movie, either a drive-in or a walk-in."

"We could do that," Amy replied. But she really

wasn't in the mood for a movie. She wanted to talk to Zach and get to know him better. In spite of what she'd heard about him being bitter about relationships, she found him quite charming.

"Or there's always cow tipping."

"Cow tipping?" She'd never heard of that.

"I was only kidding."

"What is it?"

After Zach explained how some obnoxious teenagers with more time on their hands than common sense liked to go into the fields and push over cows while they slept, Amy was shaking her head in disbelief.

"I can't believe people actually do that."

"You'd be surprised at what some bored teenagers do for fun around here," he said.

"Did you ever tip cows?" she asked, hoping he was as good of a teenager as he was adult.

"Never. I was way too busy with sports."

"That's good," she said.

"What did you do in Nashville for fun?"

Amy had been hoping he wouldn't ask that. Should she tell him she spent most of her time with her parents at the country club? Or should she say she spent almost a year working on her "Coming Out" party, where debutantes of high society walked down the center of the country club stage and were "presented" by their fathers? Not in this lifetime, she thought. Those were things people in Clearview wouldn't understand. In fact, Amy didn't even understand them, now that she saw what real life was all about.

"So, what do you wanna do?" he asked. "We need to decide something pretty soon."

"How about going back to my place for dessert and maybe a game?"

"Dessert sounds good. What kind of game?"

"Monopoly? Or how about Pictionary?"

Zach laughed. "I think we'd need at least two other people to play Pictionary. Monopoly sounds good, but I better warn you. I'm the champ."

"You've never played Monopoly with me," Amy said smugly. "I'll beat your socks off."

Chapter Ten

Zach's eyes twinkled when he laughed. "Don't count on it, Amy. I'm ruthless."

"Just watch me."

For the next four hours, they were neck and neck, both of them buying property and demanding rent from the other one as they landed on each other's squares. Amy loved the feeling of open laughter and lively banter that she'd never experienced with a guy before. Most of the men she'd been with in the past had been stuffy types who seemed afraid to let their hair down around her because of who her father was.

That was the main reason she didn't want Zach to know anything about her past. She didn't want to take a chance on him finding out that she came from blue blood stock. Clearview had been the perfect place to hide from all that, but it looked like things might change soon.

Amy won by one unlucky roll of the dice for Zach. He snorted as he gave her all the money he had left. "Looks like you're the better business person between the two of us." As he spoke, he smiled, letting her know that he wasn't upset.

"At least in the game. I wish it was this easy in real life."

"Yeah, me too."

Their gazes locked. Amy felt an unfamiliar twist in her abdomen. She longed to reach out and touch Zach's chin, but she forced herself to keep her hands by her side.

"Amy," he said after a long, long time, "I think I better go."

She nodded. "I had fun, Zach."

He didn't say anything until they reached the door. Without warning, Zach turned to Amy and took her in his arms, pulling her to his chest. She felt his breath in her hair, which felt warm and wonderful.

"I swore I'd never let another woman into my life after what happened before, but something's going on." She didn't feel his breath anymore, letting her know he'd turned his head.

She pulled away. "It's hard to forget about something if you've been hurt."

"Yes, it is," he replied, backing toward the door. "I had a nice time, Amy. Maybe I'll see you around sometime?"

She gulped and gave her head a quick tilt. This parting thing was the most difficult thing she'd ever done. He needed to get out soon, or she feared she might start crying in front of him.

The instant he backed out of her driveway, she burst into tears. Not only did she have to worry about her past coming back to haunt her and color the image she had in Clearview, she had to deal with Zach's past hurts. Amy had no idea that falling for someone could be so complicated. All the movies showed people whose biggest obstacle was an angry father or a job that kept them away from each other. This was much deeper.

At least now she didn't have to worry about whether she should invite Zach to Andrew's and Denise's house when her parents were in town. He most likely wouldn't come if she did.

She didn't hear from anyone until she went to church on Sunday. Denise was waiting in front of the sanctuary for her when she walked up.

"Well?" Denise said with an expectant look on her face.

Amy shrugged. "Well, what?"

"You know. Don't play games. How'd it go?"

"You mean the date with Zach?"

Denise rolled her eyes. "Sometimes you act so dense. If I didn't know better, I'd think you had something to hide."

"I don't have anything to hide," Amy said slowly. "But I don't have much to tell, either."

"You can start by telling me what you did."

"Not much. We just went to the Burger Barn, then back to my place for a game of Monopoly."

"Monopoly?" Denise shrieked. "You have a gorgeous hunk in your house, and all you do is play Monopoly?"

Amy nodded and looked away. She couldn't take Denise's teasing right now.

"Okay, Amster, I understand. You don't feel like discussing it right now. Just let me know when you want to talk. I'll listen."

"Yes, I know, Denise," she replied, daring to look her in the eye. "Thanks."

Andrew chose that moment to walk up to them. He opened his mouth, but Denise gave him a look only a wife could give, and he clamped his mouth shut. Amy really appreciated that.

After church, she went straight home. She knew that everyone was meeting at the Hadaways' house for their traditional Sunday afternoon meal, and she planned to go. But she needed a couple of hours alone to think.

Zach's truck was in her driveway when she arrived. What was with him, always surprising her like this?

"We need to talk," he said the instant she got out of her car. No greeting, no small talk.

Amy nodded and continued walking toward the door. She didn't want to look at Zach right now. Her feelings were raw.

Once they got inside, Zach reached out and turned her around to face him. "Mike says I'm an idiot."

Amy laughed. She didn't mean to, it just came out. "Why does Mike say you're an idiot?"

"He seems to think there's something special between you and me and that I should quit being such a bone-headed toad and let things happen."

Her breath became ragged. Amy didn't know what to think. She tried her best to look away.

Zach's hand came to her face, and he smoothed her hair back. Then, he tilted her chin up so she was facing him. "And I think he's right."

Amy was stunned speechless. Zach's face lowered to hers, at first slowly and tentatively, but then his lips came down on hers with an urgency. The kiss was short but wonderful. Amy had never experienced anything like that in her life.

"So there," Zach said.

She had no idea what to do next, so she took a step back, and bravely looking him in the eye, she said, "Now what?"

Zach shrugged. "I have no idea. This wasn't in my plan. What I feel for you is something I've been avoiding ever since Melody dumped me."

Amy nodded. "Do you want to talk about it?"

"Talk about it?" he asked, confusion taking over his face.

"I'll listen if you'd like to tell me what happened between you and . . . Melody."

"I was engaged to a woman named Melody. I

thought everything was just fine between us, but one day she told me to get lost. She gave me my ring back, and I never saw her again. End of story."

Amy let out a breath she'd been holding. "Wow! That's pretty rotten. Any idea why she did that?"

"Not a clue." He looked down at the ground, then back up at her. "Well, maybe."

"I'm listening."

"She didn't like the fact that I decided to continue being an auto mechanic after I finished college."

"So that's why you've been protecting your heart?"

"Yes." Zach was good at being blunt, something she wasn't used to.

"No wonder I didn't understand what was going on."

"You're not the only one," Zach said. "I've been trying to figure that out since the first time I laid eyes on you. I wanted to get to know you, but I tried to keep my distance. Mike and Patty both told me I was being a fool. They're probably right."

Amy smiled. "Now what?"

"I've decided I want to get to know you better, Amy."

Now it was her turn to worry about getting hurt. Zach was a wonderful, kind, good-looking man she wanted to be with all the time. He occupied most of her waking thoughts, something she'd never experienced in her life. But he didn't fit in with her world. Her father would eat him alive.

"Maybe we should just take this whole thing nice and slow," she finally said.

He looked crestfallen. "You don't want to spend time with me?"

"It's not that, Zach," Amy forced herself to say, not sure what to do now. "It's just that I'm trying to find myself now, and being with you confuses me."

"In what way?"

"Actually, in a pretty good way. I enjoy every minute I'm with you, except when you leave abruptly and I can't figure out why."

"Sorry about that." Zach touched her face with his fingertips, then bent down and brushed her nose with a featherlight kiss. "Okay, we can take it easy, but I'm not one to give up easily. At least, not until you tell me to get lost."

After he left her house, Amy slumped onto the sofa. She wasn't likely to tell Zach to get lost, but she suspected he might want to after he met her father.

Amy didn't have much time to get ready for the traditional Sunday dinner. She'd bought some rolls that only needed to be browned in the oven, thank goodness. She did that, then she went into her bedroom to change. David's nephew Jonathan was going to be there, and she always enjoyed playing outside with him. Hopefully, one of these days she'd have her own child to play with, take care of, and love.

"I thought you'd never get here," Denise whispered. "Jonathan's on high octane fuel right now, and he's about to make us all crazy." She held up an empty candy wrapper. "Gertie found this in the garbage."

Amy laughed. She knew that Denise adored the little boy, but she also knew he could try anyone's patience.

As soon as she delivered the rolls to Gertie, who'd commandeered the kitchen, she went looking for Jonathan. "I think he's out back annoying the squirrels," David said. "Take this." He handed her a few slices of stale bread.

Jonathan was in the back yard, but he was flopped over, stomach down, on the swing. He seemed to be depressed about something.

"Hey, kiddo," Amy said as she approached. "What's happenin'?"

He quickly stood up and shrugged. "Not much. I'm bored."

Amy handed him one of the bread slices, then began to pinch off tiny pieces that she tossed into the yard. Jonathan imitated her. Both of them did this in silence, and soon there were birds and squirrels flocking to get their own Sunday dinner.

"When you were a kid, did you ever think that all grownups do is talk all the time?" Jonathan asked. "No one ever wants to play with me anymore. All they do when they get together is talk."

"Where's Emily?" Amy asked. "She'd probably like to play with you."

Jonathan shook his head in disgust. "She's sleeping. All she ever does is take naps."

"Oh, but she adores her big boy cousin," Amy argued. "And I just happen to know how much you love her."

He grinned. "She's kinda cute, but she's not much fun."

"It depends on what you consider fun."

With a roll of his eyes, Jonathan made a face. "She won't even play video games with me."

Amy chuckled. "I'm sure she will in a few years when she understands them."

"But I'll be a grownup by then."

She could see his dilemma. "Have you ever tried making friends with some of the kids in the neighborhood?"

"A few of them. But they're all busy right now."

Amy really didn't enjoy the same video games Jonathan liked, but she figured it was time to give in. "Tell you what, Jonathan, I'll play one video game with you before dinner, and afterwards, I'll play another one."

His face quickly lit up. "You will? Cool! You're the best grownup here."

He ran inside ahead of her as she followed, still smiling. Jonathan had a different "best grownup" every time she saw him. Sometimes it was Denise, like when she threw a picnic or made his favorite dessert. Other times it was Bethany, like when they went to the park, and she climbed trees with him. At least Amy was glad to know that she had a turn being the "best grownup."

They had just finished their game when Bethany called everyone to the big country kitchen, which is where they chose to eat rather than the formal dining room. This used to be Gertie's house, and she said she'd never liked eating beneath a crystal chandelier because it seemed too pretentious.

David said the blessing before they filled their plates at the grand buffet they had every Sunday. Denise patted the chair next to her and told Amy to sit there.

"Okay, you've held it in long enough. What's wrong?"

Amy stared at her plate. This wasn't the time or place.

"You don't have to talk now, but I wanna know what happened." Denise's voice was soothing and kind, not as demanding as it would have been coming from someone else.

"Okay." Amy shoved her peas around on her plate as she thought about it. "Why don't you come over tonight, and I'll tell you all about it?"

Denise nodded. "No sense in keeping it all inside. If you tell me what's buggin' you, maybe I can shed some light."

After dinner and clean up, which Gertie insisted on supervising, Amy fulfilled her promise to Jonathan. He'd won the first game before dinner, but Amy got the winning point in the next game.

"Two out of three," he said.

"Okay," Amy conceded.

Then, she played as hard as she could, but he still beat her. That seemed to satisfy him.

Denise reminded her that she'd be over soon. Amy nodded and left. Hopefully, her sister-in-law would know just the right thing to say and do in her situation, since she probably understood better than anyone.

An hour later, they were sitting at the kitchen table, a pitcher of iced tea between them. Amy explained her feelings of doubt over how her father and Zach would get along, then she went on to say how she didn't feel like Zach would fit into her family's world.

"You're worrying about the wrong things here, Amy," Denise said. "Yes, I understand why you don't want to tell Zach you have more in your trust fund than he'll ever make in a lifetime. But so what?"

Amy shrugged. "I don't know. It's just that he might feel threatened."

"If he's half the man I think he is, I don't think something as trivial as money will bother him." She let out a chuckle. "In fact, he might consider that a bonus."

"I don't want that, either."

Denise set her glass down and rested her hand on Amy's arm. "What exactly *do* you want, Amy?"

"I don't understand what you're asking."

"First, you say you want Zach, but you're worried he might not like the fact that your family has money. Then, when I suggest he might not mind, you seem upset by that."

Amy nodded. "Sounds like I'm talking out of both sides of my mouth, doesn't it?"

"It sure does. And furthermore, you need to quit worrying about the things you can't control and start thinking about what you can."

"You're right."

"I have another question, Amy."

"What?"

"Have you given any thought about what kind of business you might want to start?"

Slowly, Amy nodded. "A little."

"Don't keep me in suspense." Denise shook her arm. "Tell me."

"I'm not sure exactly what yet, but I think I want to do something in the car business."

Denise looked at her with disbelieving eyes. "Now you have something to worry about."

"I know."

"Your dad will just die."

"Yes, I know that, too."

"He'll never in a million years allow his little princess to have anything to do with the car business."

"You got that right."

"When do you start?"

Amy giggled. This was just like Denise. "I'm thinking about going into business with Patty."

"Patty O'Neill?" Denise shrieked. "She asked you to go into business with her?"

"Well, not exactly. She wants to open a shop where she restores engines of vintage cars, and she's found the perfect piece of property. Only problem is, the developer doesn't want to divide it, and she doesn't have enough money to buy the whole thing." Amy talked fast; she wasn't able to contain her excitement.

"So you'll be the money person. What does she think about your idea?"

Amy shrugged. "I haven't told her yet."

"Don't you think maybe you'd better discuss this with her before you start planning anything?"

"Probably."

"I have another question."

"Okay."

"What else will you do in your business besides supply the necessary capital? Are you planning to become a mechanic?"

"No," Amy replied. "Patty has that covered. I've heard she's quite good with engines and bodies of cars. But she told me she hated working on interiors. I thought I might learn to do that."

Denise nodded. "I can see you doing that. But your father might need a little time to get used to this idea."

"I know. He's pretty picky about what he wants me doing."

"Are you sure you don't want to open a toy store or a candy shop?" She could tell Denise was teasing her, so she decided to tease back.

"My only other idea is another bookstore."

Denise laughed out loud. "I think you better stick to the car restoration business. Clearview isn't ready for another bookstore yet." She winked, then added,

"Actually, I don't think I can handle the competition from someone with such a good mind."

Amy felt more comfortable with Denise than anyone else she knew. Denise had been raised in a similar manner, but her parents had both died, and she was an only child. Although she had the financial means to support herself without working, she loved having a business, and she was very responsible. Amy considered her a role model. Plus, Denise was a lot of fun, always finding things to laugh about.

"What does Zach think about your idea?" Denise asked.

"I haven't told him yet. I thought I'd discuss it with Patty first."

"Good idea," Denise said as she stood up and grabbed the phone from the wall. "What's Patty's phone number?"

Chapter Eleven

"Not now," Amy argued. "I haven't had time to think through this yet."

"Yes, now," Denise said firmly. "You need to talk to Patty so she can start planning. Besides, I want to be here when she hears the news. Someone needs to catch her as she faints."

Amy found Patty's phone number, and Denise placed the call. She was her usual friendly self, explaining who she was and what she wanted. She left out the part about Amy wanting to be her business partner, but she managed to get Patty to commit to coming over to Amy's house in a couple of hours.

"You'll be glad you came," Denise told her. Amy couldn't hear what Patty said, but Denise laughed at whatever it was.

"I can't believe you just did that," Amy said. "I'm not sure I'm ready to talk about the details yet."

"You don't have to discuss details. Just tell her your ideas so far. She probably has a few of her own."

"You're right, as usual."

Denise tilted her head and looked at Amy through narrowed eyes. "You do want her *input*, don't you?"

At first, Amy wasn't sure what Denise had meant by that, but then it dawned on her. "Yes, of course. If we go through with this, we'll have to be equal partners."

"Good. I thought you'd say that."

For the next couple of hours, Denise helped Amy get together a business proposal. "Keep in mind, this is very sketchy," Denise said with authority. "Make sure you give Patty some room for her ideas, or she probably won't even be interested."

Amy nodded. What would she do without Denise, who always seemed to have a grip on how to do things with the least amount of effort? Denise said she had to go through a lot of systems before she figured out how to work smart.

When the doorbell rang, Denise nudged Amy toward the door. "You're on," she said. "Just remember, this has to be a win-win situation for both of you, or it won't work."

Patty stood at the door, a huge smile on her face. It was obvious that she was glad to see Amy.

"What in the world is going on?" she asked. She

glanced at Denise and said, "You're the one who called me, right?"

Denise nodded, then backed up, allowing Amy to take over. "I'm just here to listen."

Patty's puzzled expression was cute, Amy thought. She wondered if that expression would be replaced by happiness or rejection. She'd soon find out.

As Amy went through her ideas, Denise handed her the papers they'd drawn on to help her with her pitch. Patty's eyes grew wider with each new thought.

"I had no idea you'd want to do something like this," Patty finally said. "But you know I don't have the start-up capital to buy the whole piece of land *and* the equipment we'll need."

She said "we." That was a good sign. "I already told you, I can buy the land. That is, if you're interested."

Patty looked over the papers, then slowly nodded. "I have no idea where you'll get that kind of money, but so far it sounds pretty good."

Denise glanced briefly at Amy, then looked directly at Patty. "There's more." She gently kicked Amy under the table and nodded. "Now's the time to spill the beans."

Amy explained her financial situation, while Patty listened with rapt attention. She hadn't wanted to do it this way, but Denise had insisted it was the only way.

"You need to start this business with all cards face-up on the table. No secrets," Denise had said.

Amy agreed. Hopefully, she'd be able to trust Patty not to tell Zach. She wanted to be the one to do it.

"Please, whatever you do, even if you turn me down on this business offer, don't tell Zach anything about my background."

Patty looked at her with wide eyes and nodded. "I won't say a word. It's not my place to, anyway."

Amy let out a sigh of relief, while Denise winked at her and mouthed, "I told you so."

Finally, after Patty asked several questions, she stood up. "Mind if I take these papers with me? I'd like to look them over before making a decision."

"Sure," Denise said before Amy had a chance. "Go ahead. You need to make an informed decision."

After Patty left, Denise turned to Amy and hugged her. "You're on your way, kiddo."

"I'm not so sure about that. We still haven't talked to Daddy about it. He might not approve."

Denise looked concerned as she chewed her lip. "Do you need his approval?"

"I'd like to have it."

"If he doesn't approve, are you willing to go through with this?"

Amy pulled her lips between her teeth, and after a moment, nodded. "Yes, I am. My father needs to see me as an adult who can make her own decisions."

"Are you sure you don't want him financing this business?"

With a quick nod, Amy replied, "There's enough in

my trust fund for this. It's not going to take nearly as much as another business might."

Denise grinned. "I was thinking the same thing."

"Besides, I hate being indebted to anyone, especially my father."

"Attagirl," Denise said. "That's a very mature attitude. And I have a feeling he'll be very proud of you for that, too."

Letting out a deep sigh, Amy said, "I certainly hope so."

Denise left shortly after that. Amy felt so mentally and emotionally exhausted, she collapsed on the sofa. Reaching for the television remote control, she figured she might as well relax the rest of the evening. She was too tired to do anything else right now.

The next morning, Carol called her. "Would you like to take a two-day job this week?"

"Sure," Amy replied. Two days was perfect. It created a diversion, but she still had time to take care of personal business. "Where?"

Carol chuckled. "It probably seems like I'm determined to keep you in the automobile business, but that's only a coincidence."

"Is the job related to cars?"

"Yes," Carol replied. "In fact, you even know this person. You met him at the car show."

Amy's heart pounded. "I did?"

"Remember Zachary Harper?" Carol asked.

Did she remember Zachary Harper? Oh, man! "Uh, yes, I remember him."

"He needs someone to help him for a couple days this week. He's been buying cars, and his phone has been ringing off the hook with quotes." Carol paused for a couple seconds before adding, "He called and specifically requested you. He said you're a natural for this job."

Amy was flattered. "Sure, I'll be glad to do it. Where do I go?"

"Right now, he's operating out of his apartment. That's the only glitch. Generally, I don't like sending temps to work in people's homes, but he comes highly recommended, and I figured that since you knew him, you'd be able to make a decision."

Amy had been curious about where he lived, but she never imagined she'd have a chance like this to find out. "I don't have a problem with that," she said, working hard to keep her voice steady.

Carol gave her the address and simple directions. When Amy got off the phone, she squeezed her eyes shut and whispered, "Yes!"

Amy showed up at Zach's apartment complex bright and early the next morning—fifteen minutes before she was supposed to be there. She figured she might as well sit in her car and wait.

But the door of his apartment opened, and he stepped outside. Almost as if a magnet had drawn them together, their eyes met. He grinned and motioned for her to come on in.

As she got closer to Zach, she felt that shimmery feeling in her stomach and chest, making her unsure whether she'd act like the professional she needed to be. He didn't waste a single second, though, so she didn't have to worry.

"This is your desk, and here's the phone. It's been ringing every five minutes or so with people trying to sell me their cars." He thrust a sheet of paper at her and said, "These are the models I'm looking for. You'll find them in alphabetical order, and the years are listed on the left, also in order."

Amy glanced at the list and nodded. "So what do I do if they have a car that's not on here? Want me to tell them you're not interested?"

"No," he patiently replied. "You never know when something will strike my interest. Just use this blank pad to jot down information they give you on the phone. I need the model, year, color, condition, contact name, and a phone number. If I'm interested, I'll call 'em back at the end of the week."

She looked over everything and saw how organized he was. This was truly a business to Zach, and from the way it appeared, he was quite successful.

"I hope you don't mind, Amy, but I have to run errands and get to work on one of the cars I bought and put in my parents' garage."

He took a step back and gazed at her, making her insides roll. "No, of course, I don't mind," she said a little too quickly.

"There's sandwich stuff in the fridge, so when you get hungry, fix yourself something to eat."

Amy nodded. "Thanks, Zach."

"Take your shoes off if you're more comfortable." It was almost as if he didn't want to leave her there alone.

"I'll be fine, Zach. Go ahead and do what you need to do."

Zach slowly backed away, still studying her, then he turned and left. Amy knew what she was supposed to do, so she tried hard to focus on the task.

Just as he'd told her, the phone rang almost once every five minutes. By the time he got back to his apartment six hours later, she had filled almost half the pad of paper with notes about cars people wanted to sell.

"That's nothing compared to what we'll get tomorrow," he told her. "I have an ad coming out in the morning paper, and we'll get at least twice that many calls."

"I don't know how you can figure out what to buy with all this information. They all sound good to me."

"I'm very selective. People in this business won't make it if they aren't."

She gulped. After sticking her neck out and making a business offer to Patty, she thought she knew what she was doing. But now, she wasn't sure. What if she made a huge mistake and bought the wrong cars? She'd have to leave that up to Patty, since she still wasn't sure what she was doing.

Zach was right about the ad generating more phone calls. He left as soon as she arrived, since he had to finish working on the engine of the car at his parents' house. "I'll be able to handle the calls tomorrow, so unless you want to just come and hang out with me, you don't need to come back," he told her.

Amy wasn't sure if that was an invitation to come over or not, so she just nodded as he left. She'd have to decide later.

The phone rang even more than it had the day before. Her finger cramped from writing so much through the day. He'd told her to put the phone on the answering machine while she ate lunch, but she chose not to. It was always nicer to have a human voice on the phone.

That afternoon when Zach came back, she forced a smile. "How's the work coming along?"

He pointed to the door. "Go see for yourself."

Chapter Twelve

Amy stepped outside and looked down into the parking lot. There, sitting under the shade of a tree, was a lemon-yellow Cadillac with the huge tail fins.

"That's beautiful, Zach!" she exclaimed. "I've never seen one like that before."

"And you're not likely to see many more, either. It's almost extinct."

Amy knew what it was like to get a thrill over a rare old car. She felt that rush of excitement whenever she spotted one on the road, now that she'd had experience. Hopefully, her father would understand the bug that had bitten her.

"Are you coming back tomorrow?" he asked as he stood at the door between calls.

"Do you want me to?"

Zach looked at her as if was looking for an answer in her eyes. Slowly, he nodded and said, "I'd like for you to come and keep me company."

"In that case, I'll be here around lunchtime," she said. "Let me bring you something to eat."

With a huge and hearty grin, he said, "Okay! Sounds great!"

Then the phone rang, interrupting them. Amy backed away and ran to her car. She needed to get out of there before she lost her mind.

As soon as she got home, she kicked off her shoes and called Denise. "You'll never guess where I've been all day."

"Zach's apartment, you sly devil, you."

"How did you know?"

Denise cackled. "I just happen to know important people in high places."

"Carol told you."

"Bingo. So, how'd it go? Score any points with the hunk?"

"He was gone most of the day, but he asked me to come back tomorrow and keep him company."

"Well, now, that's a start," Denise said. "Have you asked him to the barbecue?"

"Denise—" Amy began before she was interrupted.

"Look, Amy, there's no point in putting it off any-more. Your father loves you, and I just happen to know that he wants you to be happy. All you have to do is tell him you're madly in love with Zach, and he'll move heaven and earth to make things right."

"I never said I was madly in love with Zach."

"You didn't have to. It's pretty obvious."

Amy groaned. "I hope that's not the case."

"Well, maybe to most people, it's not, but I'm not most people. I can read you like a book."

"That scares me, Denise."

"Don't ever be scared of me." Denise cleared her throat. "I take that back. If you don't ask Zach to the barbecue, you'll have every reason to fear me."

"Yeah, right."

"Seriously, you need to. For yourself. For Zach." Denise paused before adding, "For your dad."

"I'll think about it."

"Don't wait too long. I just happen to know that Zach keeps himself pretty busy on weekends with his cars."

"You know that?" Amy asked. "How?"

"I've been asking around."

If anyone else had told Amy that, she would have been furious. But Denise was different. She could get away with things no one else could. In fact, that was an endearing quality.

"Okay, I'll talk to him tomorrow."

"Tell him to bring the chips."

"Chips?"

"You don't think he's getting a free meal, do you? For that matter, neither are you. You bring the bread as usual, and he can bring the chips." Denise's voice of authority had taken over. "Gertie's doing dessert, Bethany and David are making potato salad and cole slaw, and Andrew and I are cooking chicken, ribs, and steak. Any special requests?"

"Uh, no." Amy's mouth was already watering. But she still felt uneasy about asking Zach to come to the barbecue. Facing her dad wouldn't be easy for anyone, let alone someone who wasn't used to his type.

"So do what I say and there won't be any trouble," Denise teased.

"Okay, okay, I'll do it."

The next morning, Amy got up, dressed in jeans and a soft, short-sleeved canary-yellow sweater, and headed for Zach's place. He'd made a pot of coffee and had a tray of pastries waiting for her.

"I was hoping you'd come," he said as he pulled out some plates and a mug for her.

They discussed the cars he'd already bought between phone calls and sips of coffee. The whole thing felt cozy to Amy. She never wanted the day to end. And she certainly dreaded the moment when Zach would meet her dad—that is, if he agreed to go to the barbecue with her.

"Something's on your mind, Amy," Zach finally said. "I've been watching you since you've been here, and once in a while, you look like you want to tell me something. What is it?"

She must have been pretty obvious. Well, she might as well ask now. "My parents are coming to stay with my brother and his wife this weekend, and they're having a barbecue." She stopped for a moment to study his expression.

"That's nice," he said with a quirky grin. "And?"

Amy shrugged and began to fidget with the corner of her napkin. "I was wondering, well, I thought . . ."

"What did you wonder?" Zach had reached out and touched her cheek with the back of his hand, sending electric currents throughout her face. She loved the way his large, callused hands could feel so soft and soothing against her skin. It was wonderful.

"I was wondering if you'd like to go." Amy licked her lips and added, "But if you don't want to go, I certainly understand. After all, my father can be quite an imposing figure. He's—"

Zach had started laughing. "Whoa, Amy, slow down. I'd love to go with you to your family barbecue. What should I bring?"

"Chips," she stated softly.

"Chips?" He grinned again. "As in potato chips?"

"Yeah, and corn chips."

"Okay. That seems like I'll be getting off easy. Are you sure you don't want me to make something? I'm a pretty good cook, if I must say so myself."

"Chips will be fine," Amy said with a nod.

Zach grinned and pulled his hand back from her face. "I'm really glad you asked me. It's been a long time since I've done something like this."

Amy smiled back as she stood up. "I really need to leave now, Zach. I have a lot of things to do at home."

"Let me walk you to your car," he said.

When he reached over to turn on the answering machine, Amy was able to take a good look at the man she loved to be with more than anyone else. He was a wonderful guy, fun and great to look at. And he was nice. So what if her father didn't think he was good enough for her? That was just too bad.

Zach gave her a quick kiss on the lips before he held her car door for her. "I'll call you later on this week," he said. "Drive safely."

All the way home, Amy's thoughts ran through her mind in a jumbled mess. On one hand, she was thrilled at the prospect of being able to show Zach off to the people she cared most about. On the other hand, though, she was scared out of her skull. She'd never cared for a man like this before. What if someone did or said something to jeopardize their relationship? It was too late to worry about that now. She'd already asked him.

Zach tried his best to keep his feelings from getting away from him. Amy had actually invited him to meet her family, something he'd vowed he never wanted to do again. It could only mean one thing. His feelings had gotten out of control for her.

But the more he got to know her, the more he realized she was nothing like Melody. Amy had a softer edge. She was refined and polished. She had class and dignity. She was sweet, too. Melody was anything but sweet. He'd been attracted to her in a completely different way, and sweetness had nothing to do with it.

Then, he thought about Amy asking him to bring chips to the barbecue. Obviously, she wasn't aware of his culinary skills. He'd bring something that would knock her socks off—and hopefully impress her family.

"You actually asked him?" Denise screeched.

Amy nodded. "Yes. Can you believe it?"

Denise took Amy by the hand and dragged her all the way inside the house. "No, but I'm glad you did. I was thinking I might have to go ask him myself."

"I know," Amy said with a chuckle. "That was my motivation. I didn't want you to do that."

With a shrug, Denise said, "Whatever works."

Andrew wasn't home yet, so Amy and Denise went into the kitchen by themselves so they could talk. The huge table she'd had delivered was shoved up into a corner, and Denise had hung a smaller tablecloth over one side of it, making a cozy spot for two people to sit. Denise had a knack for making things seem homey.

"Okay, I want details," Denise said after she placed a pot with steeping teabags between them. The cups were mismatched but complementary.

Amy told Denise all about how she'd been working for Zach and how he'd gotten scores of phone calls from people wanting to sell him their old cars. "I only worked two days, but he asked me to come back today and keep him company."

Denise offered a sly grin. "He likes you a lot, Amy. Guys don't ask women to come over and keep them company unless they have strong feelings for them."

Letting out a long sigh, Amy shook her head. "But I think it's hopeless between us. I can only imagine what Daddy will say. Zach shouldn't have to deal with it."

"Zach is a big boy, Amy," Denise said in a booming voice. "And your dad isn't that big of an ogre. He'll like him, I'm sure."

"I wasn't sure if I should warn Zach."

"Did you?"

"No. I didn't want to talk about the money thing. I was afraid to."

"Well, if you ask me, that's another thing that shouldn't matter. Zach likes you whether you're rich or poor."

"I certainly hope you're right."

Denise patted Amy on the hand. "I know I am."

They drank their tea and talked a little more about the barbecue. "You should see the new apron Andrew bought for the big event."

"He's wearing an apron?" Amy said between giggles.

Nodding and chuckling, Denise said, "Yeah, and it says 'Kiss the Cook' in big red letters."

"Daddy will probably have something to say about that."

Denise stopped laughing. "You worry way too much what your father might say. You should learn to have fun and let him deal with his own feelings."

"You're right, but it's hard. I've never been like

you. Even after I came here, I didn't have to face my father with decisions I made."

"You don't need his approval anymore. You're a grown woman, Amy, able to make decisions on your own. If you disagree about something, and you still feel that you're right about whatever it is, you need to stand up to him. He'll eventually respect you for that."

Slowly, Amy nodded. "Yes, Denise, you're right, as usual. It'll be hard, but I'll do it. I really like Zach, and if he likes me, I want to see more of him, no matter what Daddy thinks. And if the relationship goes to the next level, then it's my business, and I don't have to seek approval from anyone."

"You go, girl," Denise said, standing and picking up the empty cups and saucers. "Just remember your father loves you very much. He'll eventually come around, even if you have a disagreement in the beginning." She paused for a moment and took a deep breath that she slowly let out. "Trust me. I've been there."

"I know you have."

Amy went home with a new sense of what she was going to do. She knew it wouldn't be easy, but she had to take a firm stand in order to keep her self-respect. It was her life to lead, and even if she made a few mistakes along the way, they'd be her mistakes. And she'd learn from them.

The next day, Zach called. He told her he'd pick her up in the Cadillac to drive to the barbecue. Amy thought that sounded like fun. Gertie seemed to like old cars, and maybe she'd get to ride around the block in it. Zach told her he'd be glad to take anyone for a ride who wanted one.

Each hour that passed, every moment that drew her closer to the time she'd introduce her father to Zach, gave Amy a nervous jitter in her abdomen. Although she'd made the decision to be her own person, it was still nerve-racking even to think about it.

Finally, the day was here. Amy must have changed clothes a half dozen times before she finally settled on a pair of blue denim jeans and a pink knit top. She knew she looked best in pastels, and the scoop neck showed off her bouncy haircut better than anything else she'd tried on.

When Zach came to the door, she caught her breath. He looked absolutely fabulous. In fact, each time she saw him, he looked better.

His short hair was freshly washed and combed back. He wore a light blue polo shirt and dark khaki slacks. Amy stared at him as he stood there waiting for her to say something.

"Are you okay?" he finally asked.

"Uh, yes," she stammered. "Let me get my purse and the bread, and we can go."

When they got into his car, she smelled something. Sniffing around and finding the source of the wonderful aroma on the backseat, she whipped her head around and faced him. "You didn't have to bring anything but chips, Zach."

His face reddened. Zach actually blushed! This was

a first. "I know, but I thought I'd whip up a batch of baked beans and a corn casserole. But don't worry. I didn't forget the chips. They're in the bag."

"You know how to cook?"

"I love to cook."

Amy settled into the seat and thought about how much better Zach kept getting. Not many men in her life had known the first thing about cooking, but she didn't know why not. Her brother Andrew had never been allowed in the kitchen until the meal was served, but now Denise had him actively helping her, and sometimes he even prepared entire meals by himself. Amy had to admit, he was pretty good at it, too.

They pulled into the long driveway of the house Amy's father had insisted on buying for her and Andrew when they'd first moved to Clearview, and Zach let out a low whistle. "I had no idea."

This was the first test to see how Zach would handle her family's money. "You ain't seen nothin' yet," she said caustically.

Chapter Thirteen

Zach looked at her with a quizzical expression, but he didn't say anything. He handed her the bag of chips, and then he somehow managed to pick up both prepared dishes. Together, they walked up to the front door. He stood there in silence while she rang the bell.

"I feel like I'm in an old movie," he said while they waited for someone to answer. "Will we be greeted by the butler?"

Amy snickered. "Not if Denise has anything to do with it."

Gertie was the first one to the door. Amy figured she must have been sitting there waiting.

"Come in, come in," Gertie said as she reached out and literally grabbed the warm dishes from Zach.

Then, she winked at Amy and said, "He's quite a looker, sweetie. You really know how to pick 'em."

Gertie never hid her feelings about anything. She came out with whatever was on her mind, which made her interesting to be around. Never a dull moment.

By the time they got to the end of the foyer, they'd been joined by Denise, Jonathan, and Bethany, who all talked at the same time, greeting Zach, and pulling them to the back of the house. Zach had a half-grin on his face, and he went along with everyone.

"The guys are out back talking about setting up a game of horseshoes," Denise said.

"Horseshoes?" Zach asked. "I haven't played that in years."

"Then you'll fit right in. Andrew has never played, and David only saw someone play it once. Maybe you can teach them a thing or two." Denise's chuckle sounded warm and inviting. She had a way of making people feel comfortable, which made Amy happy.

Jonathan took Zach by the hand and said, "Come on, I'll show you how to play. I used to do it in pre-school. But these are real horseshoes, and the ones I used to play with were plastic." His voice trailed off as they disappeared down the hall, through the massive formal living room, through the kitchen, and out the back door.

As soon as they were gone, Amy turned to Denise. "Is Daddy out there yet?"

"No, he and your mom are still upstairs getting ready. Seems they didn't realize this was an informal barbecue. Andrew and I had to loan them some clothes." Denise didn't look Amy in the eye, but Amy had a feeling she wasn't going to let anything get her down.

"What did you loan them?"

"Andrew brought him some jeans, and I gave your mom a choice of several pairs of slacks and tops in various sizes. This is one time I'm glad I've been up and down the scale. I'm not sure what size she'll need."

"Daddy isn't used to wearing anything other than a business suit. I can't imagine him wearing jeans."

"He'll look different from how any of us have ever seen him, that's for sure," Denise said with a snort. "And it'll be good for him, too."

"Does he know about Zach?" Amy asked.

With a nod, Denise replied, "Yeah, Andrew told him you were bringin' a fella. I told him to let it be a surprise, but he seemed to think it would be better to have some warning."

"Does he know about Zach being a mechanic?" Amy gulped as she waited for the answer.

"Yeah, seems Andrew mentioned that."

"And what was his reaction?"

With a quick shake of her head, Denise said, "It was odd. He didn't say anything about that. Just told us he wanted you back in Nashville."

"Oh, man," Amy groaned. "He's probably furious."

"He'll get over it."

"I'm not so sure."

"At least give him a chance."

"Where is everyone?" the loud voice boomed at the kitchen door.

Amy looked up and saw her dad standing there looking uncomfortable in a pair of jeans and a T-shirt with a collar. He looked comical because of how he stood there so stiffly, but she thought she could get used to it.

"Amy?" he said. "What did you do to your hair?"

She rushed across the kitchen and flung her arms around his neck. He looked completely different, but he smelled the same. Amy took a deep whiff, allowing his familiar scent to fill her nostrils.

Her mother appeared at the door wearing a pair of navy pants and a knit top similar to her own. And she looked absolutely fabulous. The clothes took years off her appearance.

"Mom!" she shrieked, turning to pull her into the embrace.

"Amy, your hair!"

Funny how both of her parents noticed her hair and mentioned that before anything else. She couldn't think of anything to say.

Denise saved her. "She had it cut in a stylish bob. Isn't it cute?"

Her father's eyebrows went up, and he took a deep breath. Her mom forced a smile. "It is cute."

Amy knew it had been hard for her mother to say that, but she was proud of her. Her father, on the other hand, still hadn't said a word. She could handle this as long as she didn't let on that it bothered her.

"It's so much easier to take care of, Mom. You should try doing something like this yourself."

Her mother glanced at her dad, then turned back to her. "Maybe one of these days."

Once again, Denise saved the moment by motioning everyone to grab something to carry to the backyard. Gertie was surprisingly quiet, something Amy had never seen before. She just looked back and forth between Amy, Denise, and Amy's parents. Amy wondered what Gertie was thinking that kept her from talking.

Everyone had something to carry, including Amy's father. His wife was right behind him, then the rest of them followed.

Zach was standing behind Jonathan, showing him the proper form to throw a horseshoe, when he looked up and grinned. It must have been overwhelming for him to see both her mother and father for the first time, with a whole group of family and friends right behind them. But he didn't appear fazed or worried. In fact, Amy thought he looked pretty relaxed. Too relaxed, maybe.

Denise stepped forward and made the introductions. Zach thrust his hand toward her father. "Nice to meet you, sir," he said with respect.

Mr. Mitchell nodded and mumbled something. Amy's heart sank. She could already tell what he thought of Zach.

Her mom was different, though. Her smile was wider than usual, and she actually reached out to hug Zach, who looked slightly uncomfortable but flattered. He hugged her back.

Andrew stepped toward the crowd wearing his "Kiss the Cook" apron, holding a pair of tongs in one hand and a glass of iced tea in the other. "Hi, Dad," he said. "Glad to see the jeans fit."

Again, Blake mumbled something that no one could understand. Everyone exchanged a nervous glance.

Blake Mitchell was definitely out of his element for the first time Amy had ever noticed. Funny how she'd never realized he'd manipulated things to where he was surrounded by his own comfortable things. Here he was with people he didn't know, wearing clothes he wasn't used to, and seeing his son wearing an apron. That must have put him over the edge.

His wife Sue, on the other hand, seemed to be enjoying every minute of it. She laughed at everything that was said, and she hung close to Gertie, who still hadn't said much.

The guys resumed their horseshoe game with Zach being the teacher. David was a good student, listening and following directions. Andrew had a little more trouble, and he blamed it on having to worry about the meat on the grill. Jonathan was having the time of his life. Blake was the only man who stood off to one side and just watched without participating.

Finally, Gertie couldn't take it anymore. Amy watched as the elderly woman practically threw herself at Zach and said, "Move aside, fellas, let me show you how it's done."

Zach grinned down at her and handed her the horseshoe he was holding. "I bet you can, too, Mrs. Chalmers."

"Call me Gertie. Everyone else does." She took the horseshoe, held it in front of her like she'd seen everyone else do, then she stopped, turning to face Zach. "I want a lesson, young man."

"You look like you know what you're doing."

"Well, I don't," she said, turning to face the women with a wink. "I just can't stand lettin' the men have all the fun. Stand behind me and help me wrap this dern thing around that pole."

Amy had to stifle a chuckle. Gertie was playing her little game with Zach, and although it was obvious even to him, he went along with her. He fit in with everyone but her dad.

After the game was over, they ate. Amy couldn't remember food tasting so good, ever.

"Who made these delicious baked beans?" Sue asked. "I've never tasted anything quite like them."

Zach raised his hand and said, "I did. Thanks."

"What did you put in them?"

"It's an old family recipe that's been passed down."

Sue glanced over at Amy and giggled. "If you have to be part of his family to get the recipe, Amy, do it."

Heat instantly rose to Amy's cheeks. She had no idea how to react, after this comment from her mom. This was so unlike Sue Mitchell.

Blake began to cough, and Andrew slapped him on the back between his shoulders. "Get me something to drink, boy."

Amy watched Andrew hesitate for an split second, then he hopped up and grabbed the pitcher of tea. She could see that Andrew didn't appreciate the way he was being treated, but he had the sense not to create a scene in front of everyone else.

After they finished eating, Blake came up to Amy and said, "I need to have a talk with you."

"Okay, in a little while, Daddy," she replied.

"Now."

Sue stepped up to him and gently placed a hand on his shoulder. "Not now, Blake."

He turned and glared at his wife. "Now." Sue shrank back.

Amy followed her father inside to the study. As soon as the door was closed, he turned and faced her. "What is the meaning of all this?"

"Of what?" Amy squared her shoulders to show him she wasn't going to shrink like her mother just had.

"This barbecue where you eat with your fingers. This silly game of horseshoes. This auto mechanic you brought. I thought you knew better."

"Daddy, I love get-togethers like this. And I think the game looks like a lot of fun." She gulped. "And I really like Zach, Daddy. He's the nicest man I've ever met."

He made a choking sound. "I'm sure he is. Just don't get too serious about him. Who are his parents?"

"I don't know them, but he told me they have a farm on the edge of town."

"What kind of farm?"

"I'm not sure. But I do know they have horses and cows."

"Cows?" Blake shook his head. "I want you to come back to Nashville so your mother and I can look after you."

"I'm not going, Daddy." Amy reached out and touched his arm to let him know she loved him. She knew that the reason he was acting like this was because he wanted to protect her. But she didn't need his protection anymore. She was a grown woman now, and she loved her independence. "I love it here."

He held his hands up. "What's there to love?"

"My friends, the house I'm borrowing from Denise." She paused for a moment before adding, "And Zach."

"You love him?"

For the first time since she'd met Zach, she was willing to admit that she'd fallen in love with him. She nodded. "Yes, and I'm getting ready to open a business with another friend you haven't met."

"A business?" he asked, his voice deeper than usual. "What kind of business?"

Amy licked her lips. She knew this would be like the final punch in a boxing match. "Antique auto restoration."

"I won't loan you the money for the car business."

"You don't have to. I have enough in my trust fund."

He slapped his forehead with the palm of his hand. "I don't believe this, Amy. What in the world do you think you're doing?"

She stood up to him, facing him, looking him directly in the eye. "For the first time in my life, exactly what I want to do."

They glared at each other for a few seconds before Amy backed toward the door. "I love you, Daddy, and I know you want what's best for me. But I also want you to back off and let me make my own decisions for a change."

She left him standing alone in the room, feeling emotionally exhausted. When she joined her mother, she ignored everyone else's curious looks.

Sue gently placed her arm around Amy. "What happened?"

"I told Daddy that I'm ready to make my own decisions and that I'm staying here."

Tears instantly sprang to Sue's eyes, and she smiled with quivering lips. "Good girl, Amy. I'm proud of you. I know this wasn't easy, but it's time he learned to let go."

"You agree with me?" Amy whispered.

"Absolutely," Sue replied. "But it isn't easy for me, either."

Amy couldn't remember ever having so much love and respect for her mother as she did at this moment. "Thanks, Mom."

Gertie had asked Zach to take her for a ride in the car. Jonathan was with them. When they got back, Gertie's smile radiated happiness that Amy had never seen in her before. While Gertie was always smiling, laughing, and cracking jokes, she still held something back. Now, she looked positively gleeful.

"I like your young man, Amy," Gertie said as she joined the women. Then, she nudged Sue and said, "I hope she keeps him. He's a honey."

Sue smiled back. "Me, too. I like Zach."

After they cleaned up and finished playing another game of horseshoes, Amy motioned to Zach that she was ready to leave. She leaned over and hugged her mom. "I'll see you at church tomorrow." Her dad was still in the house. After their discussion, he hadn't rejoined the group.

Chapter Fourteen

All the way to Amy's house, Zach remained silent. He knew something had happened when she'd gone inside and spoken with her father, and he suspected it had something to do with him. He got the feeling Blake Mitchell didn't approve of her seeing him. Maybe he should back off and let her work through whatever it was.

When he walked her to the door of her cottage, Zach bent over and kissed her on the cheek. "I had a very nice time, Amy. Thanks for inviting me."

His heart melted when she looked up at him. He already knew he was falling in love with her, but he couldn't say anything now, especially after the incident with her father that had obviously upset her.

"Would you like to go to church with me tomorrow?" she asked.

Although he was tempted to take her up on her offer, he forced himself to shake his head. "I don't think so, Amy. Not tomorrow. Maybe some other time."

The pained expression on her face was so intense, he had to look away. It was for the best. Giving in to his feelings now would only complicate matters.

She nodded and flitted inside her house, closing the door behind her. Zach left, feeling an ache in the pit of his stomach.

How could her father have done this to her? Amy wondered. But after she thought about it some more, she remembered that he'd always had an active hand in her life. He'd guided her in her friendships, making sure she hung out with what he considered the "right" people. If he'd disapproved of some guy she was interested in, he always introduced her to someone else, someone who came from a family he'd known through business.

Andrew had been stronger than she had been. While Blake had tried to manipulate Andrew's life, too, her brother had just graciously done whatever it was he wanted to do. But she'd buckled and tried to be a good girl. And look where it got her.

She was miserable. Why didn't her father at least try to get to know Zach? If he'd give him a chance, he might discover some quality he admired.

Zach was a very strong man with convictions that impressed Amy. His business ethics were high, and he exuded warmth and enthusiasm that overflowed and impacted people he was around. Amy loved watching him work and play. He was good at both.

What confused her now was the way he held her at arms' length on her doorstep. She'd expected him to be like he was last time, but he'd set his jaw and walked away from her. That hurt.

She'd thought he felt the same way toward her that she felt toward him. Obviously she was wrong. He was downright cold when he left her.

Amy was frustrated and confused. She watched television until Denise called after everyone at the mansion had gone to bed.

"Zach's a very special guy, Amy. I think he may be the one."

"Not if today is any indication," Amy said sadly.

"Tell me about it. Sounds like you need to get a few things off your chest."

Amy spilled her guts to her sister-in-law, who listened with rapt attention. She told her about her conversation with her father, then she even admitted the brush-off at the door.

"Sounds to me like Zach picked up on some bad vibes from your dad. Want me to do something?"

"If I thought it would help, yes, but no, I don't think so." Amy bit back the tears. "I'm so confused."

"Well, if you want my opinion, I think you did the

right thing by talking to your dad. It's time you stood up to him."

That meant a lot to Amy. Denise seemed to know the difference between the right and the wrong things to do in situations like this. But that didn't ease the pain of her father's anger and Zach's apparent desire to put distance between them.

"Trust me, Amy," Denise finally said. "I know it seems bleak right now, but things have a way of working out."

"I know," she replied before they hung up. But she really didn't know. In fact, she'd never been so unsure of anything in her life.

Amy sat with Gertie in church on Sunday. She noticed a smirk on the elderly woman's face, but nothing was mentioned until services were over and it was time to leave.

"I'm disappointed you didn't bring your young man to church with you this morning." Gertie fanned herself with her bulletin. "But then I realized you might feel threatened by me. He did give me a lot of attention yesterday." She nudged Amy, then chuckled. "You know I'm just kidding, right?"

"Of course, Gertie," Amy replied. "But I also know you're pretty special. Zach really enjoyed being around you."

Gertie's expression turned serious. "Don't let anyone else tell you who you may or may not fall in love with, Amy. That's between you and your guy."

"Yes, I know," Amy replied. "But it's hard after

years and years of trying to be a good girl in my dad's eyes."

"You're still a good girl, sweetie. And no matter what, you know your dad will still love you. He's a good man, ya know. Just a little misdirected."

Amy had already come to the same conclusion. She hugged Gertie and thanked her, then left.

Patty called her later on. "I've been thinking about your offer, Amy, and I'd like to get together tomorrow. Are you busy?"

"Not yet," Amy replied. "Where would you like to meet?"

"Wanna come to my place? It's pretty easy to find."

Amy got directions, then hung up. At least she had something to look forward to.

The next morning, Amy called Carol and told her she had something to do. Carol sounded relieved when she said, "Oh, good, then I don't need to find you a temp job. Why don't you take the week off, and I can send you out somewhere next week?"

Fortunately, Amy didn't need the money, so she said, "That'll be fine."

She went to Patty's house that was a little smaller than Denise's cottage. It was slightly weathered, but it was charming, just the same. On the inside, there were posters and pictures of antique cars, obviously Patty's passion.

"Have a seat," Patty said, motioning to the futon sofa in the tiny living room. "I have something I want to show you."

She left and came back with a photo album. "Here are some of the cars I've worked on. Tell me what you think."

Amy slowly turned the pages of the album and admired all the cars Patty had restored. Then, she came to a picture of Zach. He was standing there between tall, slender Patty and a dark-haired woman wearing a very tight mini dress and a low-cut sweater. "Who's that?"

Patty looked very uncomfortable as she replied, "Melody, Zach's ex-fiancee."

It was hard for her emotionally, but Amy continued to stare at the woman in the picture. She had a completely different look from Amy, but she was gorgeous. Maybe that's why he'd turned away from her and acted distant. Perhaps he didn't consider her to be his type.

Patty explained her vision of what she wanted in her business. "We really need someone who can work on the interiors, though, because I won't have time to do it all."

"Is it too hard to learn?" Amy asked. "I was thinking I could do it."

"Are you serious?" Patty sounded absolutely delighted. "You'd be awesome at this. All you need is a good eye for detail and the desire to learn. I can introduce you to Kirk, a good friend who details one car a year. He doesn't do many, but he's the best at interiors."

"I'll pay him for his time, too," Amy said, nodding.

Patty waved off that comment. "Nonsense. He loves talking about what he does. In this business we help each other out."

"And I want to do all the business things that you don't have time for," Amy added.

"Good," Patty said with obvious relief. "I hate that end of it. If you can do the books and handle all the details to get us into shows, I'll be in hog heaven. It'll free me up to do what I do best."

Amy's heart was pounding with excitement over this new business venture she was about to get into. And Patty sounded equally thrilled about being her business partner.

When it was time to leave, Amy stood at the door. "I want you to understand that this is an equal partnership. Let me know what you need from me, and I'll do my best."

"I know you will," Patty replied. "I feel really good about this."

"So do I," Amy said before they shook hands.

Now, everything was perfect, except for two things: Zach was giving her the cold shoulder, and her father was still upset. She could talk to her dad, but she now realized she needed to take drastic action with Zach.

When Amy got home, she headed straight for her closet. Shoving all her clothes to one side, she went through each item, one at a time. "Nothing even remotely like what Zach likes," she said softly to herself. "Time for a shopping trip."

Amy didn't want to risk running into people she

knew, so she headed straight for Plattsville, where she knew very few people. It was time to take her new look to the next level.

After a couple hours, Amy had several brand-new items she never dreamed she'd ever buy. In fact, she still couldn't believe she'd bought them. But if she wanted to get Zach's attention, she knew she needed to resort to drastic measures. This was all-out warfare in the game of love.

She got home and dropped her packages on the bed. Then, she called Zach before she lost her nerve.

"Uh, Zach, I think we need to talk," she told him as soon as he answered the phone."

"Amy?" he asked, almost as if he was unsure of who was on the other end.

"Yes, this is Amy. I want to talk to you."

"Okay," he said slowly. "When?"

"Tonight okay?" she asked, knowing that if she waited, she might lose her nerve.

"I guess that would be fine. How about in a couple hours?"

"I'll be there at seven," she said, then hung up.

It took Amy that amount of time to get up the nerve and get ready for her next move. She stood on his doorstep at exactly seven o'clock, her heart pounding and feeling like it was in her throat.

Zach didn't hear the doorbell ring, but he could hear someone walking up the walkway, then stopping at his door. Maybe it was Amy. He really wanted to see her, but he didn't want to create a rift between her and her father, who obviously didn't approve of him.

He went to the door and opened it a crack to see if it was her. It was.

As he pulled the door all the way open, his chin dropped. It was Amy, all right, but she didn't look anything like the usual soft, highly polished woman he'd fallen in love with.

There, standing on his front porch, was a woman with her hair in wild curls all over her head, a skin-tight black leather skirt and tank top with a jacket to match her skirt slung over one shoulder. Her black hose showed off her perfectly shaped legs and as he looked down, he saw why she appeared to have grown overnight. She wore high heels that looked to be a good six inches, at least.

"Amy?" he asked.

She threw him a sultry look and nodded. "May I come in?"

"Uh, yes," he replied, still stunned, and stepped to the side. She reached around him and slammed the door, catching him by total surprise.

"What's going on, Amy?" he asked.

She reached out and took him by the hand. "I thought you and I had something special, but then I realized that I wasn't the kind of woman you liked. So I decided it was time to make a change."

Suddenly, it clicked. Amy Mitchell was willing to become someone she wasn't, just because she cared about him. Melody never would have done this for him.

Shaking his head, he motioned for her to sit on the sofa. "Let's talk, Amy."

She sat down, looking slightly confused and very uncomfortable. "What's there to talk about?"

"First of all, the look. Where in the world did you get clothes like that?"

"Plattsville." Her bright red lips now held a pout. He could tell he'd hurt her feelings.

With a deep sigh, he went on. "But why? I liked you just the way you were."

Amy looked around the living room nervously, then back at him like she wasn't quite as sure of herself as she was when he first opened the door. "I saw a picture of Melody."

Zach tilted his head back and blew out a breath. "I should've known. Amy, I don't expect you to be like Melody. She's not what I want."

"But I thought—"

He interrupted her. "I think I know what you thought." Zach sat down beside her on the sofa and took her hand in his. "Actually, I've fallen in love with you, Amy. Correction, I fell in love with the Amy I knew before today. And I'm terribly flattered that you'd go to this much trouble for me."

A slow smile crept across her face. "You mean I don't have to dress like this to get your attention?"

"Never," he replied.

Amy let out a breath. "I'm so relieved. This skirt is so tight, it feels like it's cutting off my circulation."

"Do you have a change of clothes in the car?" he asked.

Shaking her head slowly, she said, "No, I didn't think I'd need one."

"I've got an idea. Why don't you change into a pair of my athletic shorts and T-shirt, and we can have a heart-to-heart talk. We need to clear the air."

Zach found something that would fit her, although loosely. He waited in the living room while she went into the bathroom to change. This was something that had never happened to him before, and he wanted to make sure he didn't mess things up.

Chapter Fifteen

Amy pulled on the knit shorts that hung to her knees. The T-shirt was even bigger on her slender frame. Well, she looked nothing like Melody now, that was for sure, but he'd said he had fallen in love with her for who she was. She had to take his word for it.

When she emerged, a slow grin crossed his face. He nodded and gave her a thumbs-up. "You look terrific, Amy."

"Why thank you, sir," she said as she pulled the baggy shorts legs out and curtsied.

"Seriously, Amy, you don't need black leather to get my attention." He took her by the hand and led her over to the sofa, where they sat down beside each other, their bodies angled so they could look into each other's eyes. "Where did you see Melody's picture?"

Amy knew she'd have to tell Zach about her new business sooner or later, so she figured she might as well start now. He listened to every word she said before he finally pulled her close and kissed her.

When he released her, Amy turned his face to her and said, "Well, what do you think?"

"I think it's pretty cool." He let out a low chuckle. "But I'm dying to hear what your dad said when you told him."

"He's not happy about it at all."

Zach's eyes widened as his eyebrows shot up. "I can understand why."

Amy hesitated before she offered a shrug. "I would like for him to approve, but it's not going to make a difference as to whether or not I do this."

"Are you sure you're willing to stick your neck out and risk your relationship with your father?" Zach asked.

"I won't be risking our relationship," Amy said. "My father likes to protect me and keep me from getting anywhere near anything that might bite. But he'll love me, no matter what I do. His love for me is unconditional."

"That's nice," Zach said, turning his attention away from her.

"Zach?" Amy could tell he was thinking about something serious, but she wasn't sure what.

"Look, Amy," Zach said. "I think we should work on our own relationship right now. Don't try to be anyone other than who you are. I love being around you, and I can't imagine you thinking any different."

"I know, Zach." Amy now felt ashamed of herself, so she hung her head.

Zach lifted her face to his and lightly kissed her on the lips. "I can't believe how much trouble you were willing to go through for me. No one's ever done anything like that before."

By the time Amy left, Zach made her feel better. He promised her he wouldn't hold her attempt to be more like Melody against her. "Just don't ever do that again," he said sternly but lovingly.

Over the next several weeks, they got together every chance they had, either at her house, his apartment, or met somewhere for dinner. Amy knew she'd never meet anyone as special as Zach, and her love for him increased. But she had no idea if he was as serious about her as she was him.

One day, after she'd finished looking over the preliminary sketches of the new garage with Patty, Zach called. "We need to talk, Amy."

"When?" she asked as she shifted the phone from her hand to her shoulder. Patty was still sitting there beside her with the blueprints in front of them.

"Tonight," he replied in a terse tone. "My place."

After they got off the phone, Amy told Patty what Zach had said. "He sounded strange."

"Hmm. Zach's usually pretty even-keeled. I don't think he has big mood swings, or anything, except for once when he was—"

"I know," Amy said, interrupting her. "When he was dumped by Melody."

Patty looked at her with sympathetic eyes. Amy knew she needed to brace herself for something but she didn't know what.

She got to his place at exactly the time he told her to be there. "You're late," he said, glancing down at his watch.

"No," she said, "I'm right on time. Your watch must be fast."

"Oh, yeah, that's right. I had to guess when I set my watch this morning, I had to put a new battery in."

Amy followed a very tense and nervous Zach into the living room. What was going on? She felt her mouth go dry.

"Sit down," he said flatly.

Amy did as she was told. Man, was he edgy. "Zach, if you want me to leave and come back some other time, I really don't mind."

He quickly turned around and face her. "No, I want to talk to you now."

"Okay." Her voice came out with a squeak. Her nerves were on the edge of her skin.

"What does your father think about you going ahead with this business?"

"I haven't spoken to him since that afternoon at the barbecue," she replied.

Zach's head tilted forward, and he glared at her from beneath hooded eyes. "You've got to be kidding.

You'll be opening the shop in a month. I would have thought you'd have talked to him by now."

"I'm not worried."

"You're not? What if he tells you he doesn't want you to do this?"

"He's already told me that. I'm going to do it, no matter what. I have a trust fund that I'm able to access, and this is what I want to do. Eventually, he'll understand and be happy for me, no matter what I do."

Zach took her hands in his and squeezed them. "Even if you marry an auto mechanic?"

Had she heard him correctly? "What did you say?"

"I said," he repeated slowly and distinctly, "even if you marry an auto mechanic?"

Amy's heart pounded as she felt her eyes mist over. "What are you saying, Zach?"

He stood up and began to pace. "This isn't exactly how I'd planned to do this, but I guess it's as good a time as any."

Amy looked up at him with hopeful eyes. "A good time for what?"

Getting down on one knee, Zach held her hands once again, his gaze focused on hers. "Amy, I don't have much to offer you but my love."

A lump formed in her throat as she studied his face. She could tell this was hard for him. "And . . . ?"

He smiled and kissed her fingertips, one by one. "Will you do me the honor of becoming my wife?"

Rather than answer him with words, Amy pulled Zach into her arms and kissed him. When they parted, she felt the stinging sensation of tears in the backs of her eyes. She couldn't talk, so she just nodded.

"What's your dad gonna say?" Zach asked.

"About what, the business or our plans to get married?" Amy asked.

"He's gonna have a lot thrown at him all at once, isn't he?"

"My father's been in business for a long time. I think he can handle it."

"Are you sure you want to do this, Zach?" Amy asked on the flight to Nashville. "You don't have to go with me, you know. I've learned to stand up to my dad on my own."

"I know, but I want him to know I'm man enough to stand beside you."

Amy laughed out loud and chuckled. "Men! Who can figure 'em out?"

"Don't even try," he replied.

When they pulled into the circular drive in front of the mansion she'd grown up in, he let out a low whistle. "You grew up here?"

Amy nodded. "Pretty awful, isn't it?"

Zach arched a brow and gave her a comical look. "If you say so."

Blake Mitchell was sitting in his study waiting for them, a gesture Amy knew was to show his power more than anything. She didn't let his powerful image get in her way of happiness. She ran around behind the desk where he sat and gave him a kiss on the cheek. Then, she turned his chair around to the side so he'd look directly at her.

"Daddy, I have some wonderful news."

"Yes," Blake said, "that's what you said on the phone. Let's hear it."

Zach came around to stand beside Amy and took her by the hand. Blake looked at him, then back at his daughter.

"First of all, I've decided for sure what business I want to invest in. Before you get upset, hear me out." Then she went into the sales pitch she'd been planning for the past week after Zach's proposal.

Amy glanced over her shoulder at Zach once she was finished, and he gave her a nod of approval. Turning back to her dad, she saw the stark look on his face. He offered no sign of what he felt or thought.

After a deep sigh, she went on. "And that's not all, Daddy, Zach has asked me to marry him and I told him yes!"

This time, the color drained from Blake's face. His chin dropped, and his eyes suddenly looked tired.

"Mr. Mitchell, sir," Zach said, now taking the initiative to do something. He didn't want to stand back and let Amy do all the talking. "I love your daughter with all my heart. My goal in life will be to make her happy and to be the kind of father to your grandchildren any man would want."

Zach stepped back when he was finished and waited. Blake didn't say a word at first. He just dropped his gaze to his desk.

"Daddy?" Amy felt a heavy sensation in her chest. This wasn't anything like what she'd expected. "Are you okay?"

"Amy," he said, then glanced over at Zach. "Zach, why don't you go to the rooms that Marie has prepared for you? We can discuss this further over dinner."

Taking Zach by the hand, Amy led him to the foyer where Marie, one of the domestic workers, met them to show them where they'd be staying. Amy's old room was being renovated, so she knew she wouldn't be staying there.

Before they parted ways, Zach bent over and whispered in her ear, "I love you, Amy, but I'll understand if you change your mind."

She didn't have a chance to respond by the time he turned around and went to his room. Her world didn't seem nearly as bright now as it had only hours ago.

Chapter Sixteen

"So," Blake Mitchell bellowed, "you want to marry my daughter."

"Yes, sir," Zach replied in a soft yet deep voice. "I love Amy with all my heart and soul."

Amy watched her father steeple his fingers above his plate. She wished she knew what was coming next, but she'd never seen this side of him. The whole room was quiet, and tension mounted. She glanced over to see how Zach was handling this. He looked uncomfortable but determined to do whatever he had to do to make things right.

"Amy," her father finally said.

She quickly jerked her head around to face him again. "Yes, Daddy?"

"Tell me more about this business you want to get into."

Amy explained everything she and Patty had discussed, all the way down to the details of the real estate they were buying and how long it would take to get the garage in working order. Zach helped her where she wasn't sure about something, but she did most of the talking.

Finally, Blake nodded and offered a closed-mouthed grin. "Amy, sounds like you've done your homework." He turned to Zach. "If she needs help, will you give it to her?"

"Yes, sir," Zach replied. "I'll do anything for Amy."

It certainly sounded hopeful, Amy thought. She glance over at her father, who'd pulled back for Marie to offer him a platter of fish.

For the first time, Sue Mitchell spoke up. "It sounds exciting to me, Blake. I never would have dreamed Amy would like cars so much. She reminds me of you when you were her age. Remember that old Mustang you used to drive?"

Amy quickly turned toward her dad. "You drove an old Mustang?"

Blake cleared his throat. "Yes, but that was in my much younger days."

"Oh, come on, Blake," Sue urged, a wicked grin on her face. "Tell them how you gave it up because someone told you we were too old for that sort of thing." Sue turned to Zach and said, "Blake was never one to call attention to himself."

Amy could tell that Zach was holding back a snicker. This was all news to her.

"Daddy, I love old Mustangs." She glanced at Zach and felt the blood rush to her face before she continued. "Uh, Zach, I'm the one who bought Mike's car."

"You?" he screeched. Then, he nodded as a look of understanding crossed his face. "So that's why you seemed so smug when he said the deal went through. Why didn't you tell me?"

"Well," she said. "I wasn't sure how to."

"Let's talk about that later," Zach said.

"I have a picture of me sitting in it, Daddy," Amy told her father.

Sue spoke up. "Show us later. Your father has something else he'd like to tell you two."

All faces turned to Blake, who looked very uncomfortable. He glanced down at his untouched plate, them back to Amy. Was that a tear in his eye?

"Amy, I have always adored you. You're my baby, and that will never change. I want to protect you from all the evils of the world." He cleared his throat before he went on. "And that's why I'm happy you've found someone like Zachary."

For the first time since Amy got back home, she was speechless. She turned to Zach, who was sitting there with his mouth hanging open.

Sue giggled. "Your father and I both approve, sweetheart. But you have to admit, this was pretty sudden. I'm sure we'll get used to the idea of a having a grown-up, married daughter eventually. In the meantime, you'll have to excuse us for our little slip-ups when we forget."

Zach stood and held up his glass. "I'd like to propose a toast to everyone in this room." He waited until everyone had their glasses elevated before continuing. "May we all get along and have a happy life together."

Blake stood up, relieving Zach from his position. "And may you produce a bunch of grandchildren for me to spoil and coddle as I get older."

As they concluded their toast, Amy realized how fortunate she was. In her wildest and most vivid dreams, she'd never imagined herself sitting in her parents' home, laughing and talking with them as their equals. And it had taken falling in love and becoming a businesswoman to make it happen.

Zach's gaze pulled her attention like a magnet. As they looked into each other's eyes, she knew they were both thinking the same thing. Everything had worked out even better than they had hoped. Their love for each other had taken them to a place neither of them had imagined.